GHOSTING
MY
FRIEND

GHOSTING MY FRIEND

A FUNDERBURKE AND KAIMING MYSTERY

CHRIS CHAN

LEVEL
BEST BOOKS

Once again, to my parents Drs. Carlyle and Patricia Chan
And to John Pittman, in memoriam

Contents

Introduction

By Isaiah Funderburke

My name is Isaiah Funderburke. I'm the Student Advocate at Cuthbertson Hall, a K-12 school in Milwaukee, Wisconsin. I started out my working life as a lawyer, but soon after getting my law degree, my actions led to the exposure of corruption in the family court system, the bankruptcy of one of Milwaukee's most prominent law firms, and the destruction of over a dozen previously sterling legal careers. In my defense, everybody who got caught up in the fallout was totally shady and deserved what they got, but try telling that to any firms that might otherwise be interested in hiring a brash young lawyer. With a lot of influential people blaming me for the carnage and refusing to concede the righteousness of my actions, I found myself incapable of finding a job in my chosen profession. After three months of not quite making ends meet as a barista, a lucky chance led to my getting hired at a small private investigation agency, where I had just enough time to learn the basic skills of the trade and get licensed before my much-missed boss succumbed to alcoholic hepatitis.

After a brief but similarly unsuccessful search for work, a miraculous turn of events rescued me. A couple of wealthy benefactors at my alma mater, Cuthbertson Hall, realized that the student body needed someone in their corner, as an unsettling number of young people were struggling due to their parents' divorces, dangerous home situations, addiction, crimes, and all sorts of other terrible problems. That led to the funding of the position of the student advocate, someone the students could turn to when nobody else was there to help them. Given my background, and the fact that I am a Cuthbertson alumnus with a lot of friends and allies amongst the faculty and staff, I finally managed to obtain a steady job that I love.

Over the years, I've been involved in a lot of interesting cases, but for various reasons, including limited time and people requesting—or demanding—privacy, I've only managed to write a few brief accounts of some of my notable adventures. Now that I've finally had the time to write a full account of probably the most personal investigation of my life, the world will at long last know the details of a case involving one of my best friends from childhood.

I dedicate this book to the memory of my late friend, Bertie Godspeed, who was taken from us far too soon and who is still much missed. This one's for you, Bertie.

–Isaiah Funderburke

Chapter One

No Answers

"I want those filthy, corrupt, lying, twisted, sick, miserable pieces of garbage in jail, Mr. Funderburke. A really, really terrible jail. The kind that Amnesty International protests. One where you never see the sun, where the food is moldy, the mattresses are a half-inch thick and filled with sand, the guards take out their frustrations over their personal and professional problems on the inmates, and everybody can watch you use the toilets that usually don't work. Can you make that happen, Mr. Funderburke?"

I tried to resist a smile, but I couldn't. The edges of my mouth raised up so high they nearly grazed my eyebrows. "Unfortunately, Nadine, divorce lawyers rarely suffer any consequences for their misdeeds. I'd love to help change that, but there are no guarantees. Maybe nothing will happen, maybe they'll get a slap on the wrist. Disbarment is possible, but it's not as common as I'd like. If there's absolutely incontrovertible evidence of professional misconduct, that may lead to a revocation of a law license, if you file an official complaint and everything goes your way. I'd be happy to help you with that."

"I'd appreciate it, thanks." Nadine leaned forward. "Are you sure that they won't be going to jail?"

"It's unlikely that they will see the inside of a cell."

"But you'll help me with the professional misconduct complaint?"

"Absolutely." Having been the victim of six malicious and utterly baseless professional misconduct complaints myself, and having come out of each one smelling of roses, thereby leaving my scheming accusers reeking of the odor of the sewers, I have a bit of experience with disciplinary proceedings for attorneys.

"Good, that's really good." The satisfaction positively radiated from Nadine's face. "Do you have the evidence?"

"Take a look." I handed her my tablet and clicked the file with the best photographs. "The subjects in question were making absolutely no effort to hide their relationship."

Nadine flipped through the photos, triumph dancing in her eyes. I don't care much for furtively taking photographs of unpleasant people, but all jobs require doing a few things you don't enjoy, otherwise, they'd be play and not work. I, therefore, sacrificed a weekday evening snapping shots of a libidinous couple going in and out of an inexpensive motel.

"And they didn't see you?"

"Oh, no, they did. It's hard for someone my size to hide, and I didn't feel like trying to disguise my presence anyway. Your father's divorce attorney and your mother's divorce attorney caught me as I took shots of them making out on their way back to their cars, and I hurried back to my car because I didn't want to talk to them. I have a distinctive face, and apparently, they recognized me—I've been on the local news, and my picture's been in the paper enough. Although, come to think of it, I wouldn't be surprised if Milwaukee's top divorce lawyers leave a photograph of me with their receptionists and tell them not to allow me inside their offices under any circumstances. They showed up in my office this morning, both full of venom and threats. I don't need to repeat them. You shouldn't be exposed to that level of vulgarity at your age. Nothing particularly original on the recording, anyway, but it's probably useful if it's parlayed right. I'll email you an MP3 of what they had to say. I started recording as soon as they started pounding on my door."

"And that's admissible as evidence, Mr. Funderburke?"

"Well, it's perfectly legal to record a conversation in Wisconsin if one of the involved parties gives consent, and I certainly gave myself permission to record everything. That abominable pair threatened my livelihood, my reputation, and my genitals. I let them snarl for a while, and told them that I had something that they'd really like to see, and if they would just wait a moment, I'd be back with it. I asked them not to say anything or move until I got back. It wasn't my fault that they started talking and trying to break into my locked desk and file cabinets, as the video surveillance proves. As they talked to each other, they managed to mention at least a dozen highly unethical actions they'd committed, if my count is correct. I suggest that your parents find someone reputable—if they can—to look into those accounts they've set up to organize their finances during the divorce because, from what I heard, their lawyers have been dipping into the till. Not only that, but they took an unearned share of the proceeds from the boat your father was forced to sell, and they mentioned lying to your parents on multiple occasions. And this was only in the five minutes I recorded. Who knows what else they've been up to in their pursuit of their forty percent?"

"Forty percent of what?"

"In the divorce industry, Nadine, unscrupulous attorneys try to figure out exactly how much their clients are worth, and then they drag out the proceedings, rack up all sorts of charges, and keep the gravy train running until they get at minimum forty percent of their clients' entire estate. For a lot of predators, forty percent is just the minimum. I'd say that this pair is out for everything they can get, and I don't think that your parents are the first to fall victim to them. I've done a little digging, and so far, I've found four other couples who have either divorced or are currently in the process of divorcing and are being tag-teamed by this unholy pair. Posing as adversaries and bilking divorcing couples who are too furious with each other to realize they're being robbed blind."

Nodding, Nadine set my tablet back on my desk. "This is wonderful." She paused for a few moments, looking like she was debating whether to say what she was thinking or not, before finally taking the plunge and asking the question that she was unjustly embarrassed to ask. "Mr. Funderburke, now that they know how they're being exploited… do you think that there's any chance that my parents will… you know…"

When it became clear that Nadine wasn't going to finish that sentence, I gently said, "get back together?"

"Well, yeah."

I shrugged, trying to be sensitive to her feelings. "That's the dream. I hope it works out for you and your family, I really do. I'd love it if there were a reconciliation. There just aren't any guarantees. At least in this case, your parents claimed to have just drifted apart, and so far as you and I know, neither one has met anyone else yet. With a little luck, these revelations will make your parents a lot less likely to trust the divorce courts in the future, and they'll be a lot more careful with what happens to their money." It's been my experience that divorcing parents are often able to justify the trauma inflicted on children by divorce by dismissing everything as being "for the best," but once someone starts messing with their money, all heck breaks loose. "If I remember P.G. Wodehouse's *Right Ho, Jeeves* correctly, "it is a recognized fact… that there is nothing that so satisfactorily unites individuals who have been so unfortunate as to quarrel amongst themselves as a strong mutual dislike for some definite person." Maybe having a common enemy in their divorce lawyers will spark a reconciliation. Maybe not. We can't tell, but I hope it works out for your sake. Just remember, Nadine, I'm on your side in this, and unlike 99.9999% of the children who are fed into the meat grinder that is the divorce industry, you have a trained and knowledgeable advocate on your side who loves a good fight."

Hope flickered in Nadine's eyes. You don't often see that in kids going through what she is. "Thank you, Mr. Funderburke. I'm going to let this sink in for a bit, and I'll talk to you soon about how I want to proceed." We said our goodbyes, and Nadine picked up her backpack and headed for the door. As soon as she touched the handle, she stopped and turned toward me. "Mr. Funderburke? You said that you had something to show my parents' divorce lawyers, which is why you left the office. What did you show them?"

"Oh, that. I went around the corner, checked the cameras with my phone to make sure they were rummaging through my office just like I thought they would, and when it looked like they'd tired themselves out, I strolled back in, pulled out the same tablet you just held, and showed them a YouTube video of a big dog out in the rain who's letting three little kittens walk underneath him because they freak out if they get even a little bit wet. It's adorable. I laughed so hard when I saw it, I thought I should share it with someone else. Well, neither of my uninvited guests were amused, and it was only by swiftly raising my tablet over my head that I was able to prevent it from getting smashed. I was glad to see that revolting couple go, and I hope that they both get what's coming to them."

Nadine agreed, and as she walked out of my office, she nearly bumped into Zita Godspeed, who was standing outside my door. The girls exchanged their "excuse mes," and Zita stepped into the room and asked, "Mr. Funderburke? Do you have a few minutes, please?"

"For you, Zita, always. Have a seat." I told her.

Zita shuffled into the room, and with a bit of difficulty, she managed to wriggle up into the chair opposite my desk. She's small for her age, and even though she's a seventh grader, she's frequently mistaken for being in the fifth grade.

I gestured towards the little table where I keep my treats. "Would you like anything, Zita? A cookie? A piece of fruit? A granola bar?" Zita happily accepted a cookie from the jar, and declined the offer of anything to drink. Taking a sip from my aluminum water bottle, I asked her how she was doing.

"Not very well, Funderburke." Normally, students are expected to refer to me with a "Mr." before my last name, but all of my close friends just call me "Funderburke," and the Godspeeds are like family to me, so Zita can take the liberty of dropping the "Mr." when none of her peers are around.

"What's wrong? Is your mother okay?"

"No. Mom's in bed with a terrible headache, and Dad's really out of it, too. The news has really shaken them up, and I can't blame them one bit. It's really upsetting, and I thought you should know, seeing as how you and Bertie were such good friends."

I felt a weird, uncomfortable feeling shoot through my stomach that was half icy wind and half electrical shock. "What about Bertie?"

"Some policemen came to our house yesterday."

"Is this about the murder? After all these years, have they finally figured out who did it?"

"No, no, sorry. It's not that. Somebody's ghosting him. At first, I thought they were talking about ignoring him on social media, but that's impossible. It's another form of ghosting. Someone's stolen his identity, and they're making a lot of money from it."

Physically, I froze. All of my muscles clenched, and I found myself incapable of either speaking or moving. Mentally, my brain was running at the rate of a thousand miles a minute. I think that my temporary paralysis must have lasted rather longer than I thought, because I was brought out of my thoughts by Zita, who had left her chair and was now tugging at my sleeve.

"Funderburke? Are you all right?"

It took a little while for me to snap out of my haze, but I managed to reply before she ripped my suit jacket. "I'm fine. I just slipped away for a minute."

Zita did not look convinced when I described myself as "fine," but she simply nodded and returned to her chair. I stumbled over to my mini-fridge, grabbed a cranberry seltzer water, and drained the contents with unsettling rapidity. The sudden intake of carbon dioxide burned my throat and nasal passages, but this brief discomfort was enough to snap me out of my daze.

Feeling more like myself again, I adopted an all-business attitude. "When did you find out about this, Zita?"

"Last night. A couple of police officers came to our house, and started explaining the situation. Unfortunately, my parents realized I was in listening to the conversation after just a few minutes, and they made me go up to my room, so I didn't get many of the details."

"Could you please tell me what the police said? Using their exact words if possible."

"Sure. The police knocked on our door not long after we finished dinner. They introduced themselves, but I can't remember their names. I'm sorry."

"Don't worry about it, Zita."

"Thanks. They were very sensitive to us, very polite. They asked Mom and Dad to prepare themselves for some distressing news. They asked my parents to confirm that they'd lost a son named Bertie about fourteen years ago. I saw Mom grabbing Dad's arm, and Dad started holding his breath…I think

6

they both thought that the police had finally caught his killer. The detectives realized this, and they told us—really apologetically—that they weren't with Homicide, and that they had no information regarding the murder. They weren't even from Milwaukee, though I'm not sure where they work. They were here because identity thieves had learned some important details about Bertie and were ghosting him." Zita paused and leaned back in her chair. "That's when Mom realized I was there and asked me to go up to my room. I didn't want to, but I could tell from the looks on their faces that it wasn't a good time to argue."

I nodded. "This can't have been easy for them."

"I guess not. So I went upstairs, and I put my ear to the floor and tried to listen, but I couldn't understand a word they were saying. Later that night, after the detectives left, I asked Mom and Dad what was going on, but they asked me really gently if I'd please just wait for a while, because they were dealing with something really overwhelming right now, and they couldn't talk about it that night. And they told me not to ask them again in the morning, either. They both looked like they'd been hit by a truck, and I was so concerned about them I knew I shouldn't say anything at all. So I didn't, and I've been thinking about it all day. A couple of my teachers asked me where my head was today. I told my science teacher if I knew, I'd tell her. She thought I was being fresh with her at first, but then she looked me in the eyes and knew something was up. I wanted to talk to somebody, but I didn't think any of my friends could help, and then it came to me. You! I should come talk to you! So here I am."

"Thanks for coming. You're going to have to be patient with me. You can see that I need to process this news myself."

"Yeah, I can tell." Zita didn't look pleased. "I know this is kind of upsetting for you, too, but it'd be great if you could focus and answer some of my questions, please?"

I may be the Student Advocate, and Zita's like a little sister to me, but I am not a fan of being sassed by a seventh-grader. The better angels of my nature reminded me that she was going through a difficult time, and I needed to cut her some slack. "Of course. I don't know what I can tell you, though. I only know what you just told me."

"But you know a lot about crimes, right? Can you explain ghosting to me? I know that it's got something to do with identity theft, but other than having something to do with dead people, I don't know what it means. I looked it up online, but after a couple of pages of search results that were all about ignoring people on the Internet, I gave up."

I have a pretty good background in solving identity theft cases. Before Cuthbertson Hall hired me, I managed to help three unconnected senior citizens who'd been victimized by people taking out loans and buying stuff in their names. In each case, the culprits were relatives who were exploiting their loved ones. "This form of ghosting is a type of identity theft that piggybacks off a dead person. In its usual form, the criminal finds the name of a deceased person. Often, it's somebody who passed away quite recently, but depending on the nature of the fraud, people who passed away long ago may be targeted, too. The crook gets the late person's name, social security number, address, birthday, mother's maiden name… anything that might be used for identification. What happens next all depends on what the criminal intends to do with it. A lot of them just take out credit cards, or maybe loans."

"How do they do that? Don't they get caught?"

"Well, a lot of credit card companies don't dig all that deeply into their applications. If someone wants to sign up for a card with a sky-high interest rate, the companies figure that the odds of profiting are way higher than the chances of losing money, so they approve the card. That's not entirely fair. Some credit card companies are quite scrupulous, but there are a few that approve first and ask questions later. So, after getting approved, the crooks then buy everything they can get their grubby hands on until they max out their credit limit, and then usually, they abandon the card and move on to a new one. That's one method. There are others. Of course, sometimes it's not so much about money as it is about assuming the identity itself."

"Does that happen often?"

"I don't think actually living under a dead person's name is common, but I don't have statistics. Anyway, if someone's in trouble with the police or something like that, and needs a fresh name and a fresh start, they can assume the identity of someone who died long ago, and pretend to be that person. Suppose a con man named John Doe is being tracked down by the authorities. Doe finds out that a kid named Robert Smith was born around the same time he was and had some similar physical characteristics. Doe gathers up the basic information on Smith, manages to cobble together some paperwork and IDs under Smith's name, and then goes about living life under the new moniker. It's often less trouble to take over the identity of someone who already existed, since there's already genuine information out there that can be used to get mortgages and insurance and all sorts of other things. The downsides are it's always possible that someone will find out that the real Robert Smith passed away decades earlier, or the family and friends of Robert Smith discover that there's an imposter using their loved one's name."

Zita looked disgusted at the perfidy of scammers. "So that's what going on? Someone's using my late brother's name as a way to make some quick money? Or maybe some lowlife's using Bertie's identity to hide from the cops?"

"Those are certainly possibilities. Maybe there's something else at play here, but I have no way of knowing without more information."

We said nothing for a little while. I didn't know how to transform the thoughts racing through my brain into intelligible sentences. At that moment, the best words to describe my emotions were "smoldering, explosive rage." The wound in my soul caused by Bertie's murder had never come close to healing, and it had only festered over the years due to the fact that it had never been solved. Having no answers as to who caused my best friend's death was bad enough, but to have his memory be further disrespected by some miscreant defiling his good name and assuming his identity caused me to fantasize about lifting up my desk and hurling it through the wall, creating a jagged yet satisfying hole. The fact that the wall is composed of thick concrete bricks had no effect whatsoever upon my daydream.

"Funderburke? Funderburke?" I don't know how many times Zita said my name, but judging by the way she was screaming it so loudly, she must have been trying to get my attention for quite some time. I was still suffering from the inability to form coherent words, so I simply made eye contact with her to let her know that I hadn't gone completely brain-dead. "I have to get back to class. My study hall's going to be over in ten minutes, and it takes me almost that long to walk back to the Middle School from your office."

I nodded, and I'm pretty sure I said something that was meant to be reassuring, though I can't for the life of me recall what sounds my vocal cords managed to generate. After Zita wriggled out of her chair, she looked up at me and asked, "Are you going to be okay, Funderburke?"

I probably overdid the casualness of my tone. "I'm fine. Don't worry about me. Just go back to class."

She nodded. "Will you give my parents a call, please? I know they'd like to hear from you. Feel free to tell them everything I told you. I don't care."

"That's an excellent idea. I'll call your mother as soon as you leave."

"Okay, good. Thanks, Funderburke."

As the door creaked shut behind Zita, I fished my phone out of my pocket, scrolled to Mrs. Godspeed's number, and dialed. I didn't have to introduce myself when she answered the phone, as presumably, she saw my name on caller ID. "Isaiah? I wondered if Zita would talk to you today. Did she tell you everything that happened last night?" There are only five people in the world who call me by my first name. Even my girlfriend Nerissa addresses me as "Funderburke." I changed my last name the day I turned eighteen to rid myself of a moniker that no longer fit me, and I was going by "Funderburke" long before it was my legal last name, but Mr. and Mrs. Godspeed have known me since I was in the first grade, so to them I'll always be "Isaiah."

"I don't want to upset you, Mrs. Godspeed. If you want to be alone, please just tell me and I'll leave you be. I felt like I ought to make the effort to reach out. I think you understand."

"Of course I do." Her voice was warm and reassuring, and I abruptly realized both that she was comforting me rather than vice versa, and that I was totally fine with it. In retrospect, I suspected that my voice might have been faster and, as much as I hate to admit it, a trifle more quavering than I would have liked. Mrs. Godspeed has excellent maternal instincts.

"Isaiah, tell me everything that Zita told you, please." I provided Mrs. Godspeed with all of the information she requested, grateful that Zita had explicitly released me from any concerns over confidentiality. When I'd finished, Mrs. Godspeed told me that Zita had overheard pretty much everything that was relevant to knowing what happened, other than the facts that the detectives were actually from Chicago and were named Boughan and Firmin, that some credit cards had been taken out in Bertie's name, and that they were polite men, though they were admittedly pessimistic about the chances of tracking down the people behind it, and in any case, this was unfortunately not terribly high on their list of priorities, but they were doing their due diligence anyway, just in case there might be some silly mistake that would lead to the perpetrator.

After thanking her for these additional details, I asked Mrs. Godspeed again how this incident was affecting her.

"It doesn't seem quite real to me at the moment, to tell the truth." Her tone was very soft and sad, and I felt a renewed surge of bitterness towards the identity thieves who were exploiting this kind woman for ill-gotten cash. "I dream about this all the time, you know. Two, three times a week, I have a dream where I'm going about my business at home, and then there's a knock at the door, and I open it to find a detective standing there, telling me that after all these years, they've finally found the man who shot my little boy. And the killer's made a full confession and pled guilty, so I don't have to worry about going to court or parole hearings down the line, he'll be in jail forever. It's done." There was a sudden crack in her voice, and I knew at once that she was crying very softly now. "After the detective leaves, everything seems brighter. In this recurring dream, it's often nighttime at the start, but once I hear the good news, the sun is suddenly shining, there's colorful flowers blooming in the yard, and my heart's a hundred pounds lighter, and I frequently start to sing. It's a wonderful feeling. The problem is, I usually wake up not long afterwards, and I think about how incredible it is that my son's killer is finally behind bars…and then I piece together everything in my head, remembering that I've had this dream so often before, and none of it was real…I think you can guess how I feel then, Isaiah."

I could. I told her I'd had similar dreams on multiple occasions, and when I awoke to realize that justice was still not done, I wanted to put my foot through the nearest door. I've never gone through with that level of destructive kicking, though.

"How's Mr. Godspeed?"

"Not bad. Not good. He's just hurting, though he hides it better than I do. He doesn't like to show his emotions. Sometimes that annoys me, but right now, I'm rather glad that he's not talking about the matter. I can't explain why, but I just don't feel like discussing this news with him right now. But I'm relieved that you called, Isaiah. Talking about this with you is cathartic for me."

"I'm glad to hear that."

"We all need to have dinner again soon. It's been three months since we last saw you and Nerissa."

I promised to check with Nerissa about her schedule and set up a time, and after a few awkward, halting goodbyes, I hung up, leaned back in my chair, and let my mind wander.

I have no desire to repeat all of the thoughts that floated through my hyperactive and mildly disturbing mind. Most of what overstimulated my synapses is simply not worth putting to paper and is best forgotten. There are a few points that I do believe ought to be recorded for posterity.

When I first stumbled into the private detection business and started to realize that I wasn't half bad at identifying liars, cheaters, thieves, frauds, and the occasional murderer (I freely admit, however, that modesty is not one of my stronger attributes), my more perceptive readers may be wondering why I never decided to put my skills to use by trying to figure out who killed Bertie. The short answer is I did, and I failed miserably. I'd never tried to look into a cold case before, and I quickly realized that such crimes are usually unsolved for a good reason. Trying to figure out who shot my best friend during a botched robbery at a corner shop a block from his house proved far more challenging than I expected. Over the course of a month, I tried to track down witnesses, only to realize that the shopkeeper at the murder scene, the one supposed witness to the crime, had died of a heart attack five years earlier. In any case, the shopkeeper, according to a news report, had fainted as soon as the masked gunman entered and was unable to provide any useful information whatsoever.

I have a handful of friends and contacts in the police department, but none of them were able or willing to help me out by allowing me access to the official case files, though a few of my so-called buddies told me that the case was hopeless. The security camera didn't even manage to capture the actual murder, for it only recorded grainy footage of an unidentifiable figure with a gun running in and out of the shop. One of my allies informed me that the shop had used and re-used the same VHS tape for the past eight years, so what little imagery they had was of exceptionally poor quality. I did get to see the tape. Due to the angling of the camera, all I could see was a hooded figure firing the gun. It didn't show Bertie's death. I'm actually glad I didn't have to see that. It did show that right after the killer turned and fired the gun, he ran towards where Bertie fell, tugged at his arm (the only bit of him that was visible in the video), presumably in a failed attempt to take his wristwatch, and twenty seconds later, sprinted for the door. At no point was the killer's face visible. The crime scene itself was long gone, knocked down and replaced with a community center. As far as I could tell, there were no witnesses, no forensic evidence, no one to interview, nothing to analyze, and no suspects. Whoever rushed into that store and stole Bertie's life was probably some random thug or drug addict out for a quick score, and ran out with nothing but blood on his hands.

After blowing four weeks of spare time knocking on doors, making phone calls, and even sitting in a library basement scrolling through microfilms of newspaper reports of the murder, I was forced to come to the same conclusion as the police: that there simply was nothing whatsoever to go on with the case. I also realized that if I was teetering on the brink of obsession, and that I'd already let Bertie's murder swallow up my life for the better part of a month. I grudgingly admit that I have an obsessive streak, which I hold is a virtue in many cases. It was Mr. and Mrs. Godspeed that who confronted me, telling me that no good could come from frittering away my precious time hunting down leads that didn't exist. So I stepped away, and very reluctantly chalked my investigation up as a miserable failure, and asked Bertie, wherever he was, to forgive me for failing him. At least some good came out of my fruitless sleuthing. For over a decade, I'd resented and loathed the homicide detectives who'd investigated Bertie's murder, believing them to be loathsome incompetents. Having done no better than they had, even though I'd lacked many of their advantages, I was properly chastened, and admitted that they'd done the best that they could with a poor set of circumstances.

Though the chances of solving Bertie's murder were slim to none, I toyed with the idea of trying to track down the criminal who had stolen his identity. I really wanted to catch the guy myself, but the calm and rational part of me (which is a terrible killjoy), patiently informed the impulsive and reckless part of me (which is way more fun at parties), that this was a job best left to the police, and that interfering in an open official investigation is strictly forbidden. I conceded the point to my stodgy and rule-abiding side, and meekly accepted the fact that it was time to do something I hate doing: nothing.

Realizing that I had spent enough time trapped in the confines of my own head, and feeling like the owner of an antique shop who wakes up on the floor of his store one morning after downing an entire bottle of tequila, and wonders where all of his Ming vases are and what these little white shards are doing everywhere, I decided to get out of my office and take a walk to clear my mind. I had so many questions, and no answers to them. That is not a situation in which I like to find myself.

In light of what happened over the course of the next several days, I sometimes look back and ask myself if I should have forced myself to be content with not having any answers. Should I have just let the whole matter lie? I only wonder about that for a few seconds. If I had just let the matter rest, I wouldn't be me.

Chapter Two

An Awesome Friend

"Funderburke, what happened to you? You look like hell."

Normally I would have retorted with a cutting rejoinder, but A) I figured Nerissa was right, and B) Nerissa was looking at least twelve different kinds of amazing that afternoon. Nerissa has very bold fashion tastes, and her wardrobe selections run towards the shiny and glossy. Her cupboards and closets are filled to bursting with silks and satins, glittering sweaters, metallic dress suits, and an entire herd's worth of leather and suede items. Not long after we first met in high school, many years before we started dating, one night at a group study session, I abandoned all prudence and told her that her clothes said "look at me," but her face shouted "but don't touch me." Her glare in the immediate aftermath of that remark is forever seared in my memory, but so is her laughter from a few seconds later, when she broke down in giggles and eventually conceded the truth of my remarks once she regained her breath. From that point on, we were the best of buddies for over a decade until, by some miracle, I managed to break out of the friend zone.

I'm not going to go into our entire relationship history here. I will say that after three seconds of gazing at her and the iridescent mother-of-pearl-colored blouse and the burnished calf-length skirt she was wearing, I was feeling considerably better.

"Funderburke? What's up? You were fine at lunch."

I waved my hand in the direction of a chair, sat down across from her, and gave her a concise account of my conversation with Zita.

When I'd finished, Nerissa leaned forward and placed her hand on my shoulder. "That explains why you were making that face you always do when you're having an internal tantrum."

"Yep."

"Do you want to talk about it some more?"

"No. But I should. I need a change of scene. Gurty's?"

"Definitely. You go on ahead, see if you can get us a couple of the comfy chairs. I'll pack up my books and today's quizzes and meet you there in five minutes." Nerissa took a quick look through my office window to make sure no students were looking in, briefly pressed her lips against mine, and left my office with a smile.

It didn't take long for me to gather up my things, pull on my lambskin walking coat, and drive my fifth-hand thirty-one-year-old Volvo the half-mile from Cuthbertson Hall to Gurty's. I can afford a newer car, incidentally. I just have a lot of sentimental attachment to my current—and still very reliable—set of wheels, which I bought with exactly five hundred dollars of money I earned from summer jobs when I was seventeen.

Gurty's is a frozen yogurt shop that specializes in all-natural, non-fat, low-sugar soft serve that actually tastes fantastic. Fans of the classic sitcom *Cheers* will remember the recurring gag where George Wendt would stride into the bar, greet people with a genial "Good afternoon, everybody!" and everybody else would shout "Norm!" I go to Gurty's often enough that I get a similar response when I walk inside.

The store was pretty crowded, as it usually is shortly after school ends, but I managed to find a couple of free comfortable chairs in a corner by the window, and I sat and waited for ten minutes before Nerissa arrived.

"Sorry I took so long," she apologized as she tossed her maroon leather trench coat onto her chair. "Fiona's having problems with her ex-boyfriend and I had to give his parents a call and tell them to set the little deadbeat straight. Not in those words."

"You really look after your girls."

"Someone has to." Nerissa is in charge of a program that provides scholarships for pregnant girls and teen mothers to come to Cuthbertson. She helps them with everything from reconciling with estranged parents, to managing both homework and parenting duties, to losing the baby weight, to handling boyfriends who aren't prepared to take on fatherhood, to finding adoptive parents. At that time, there were about a dozen girls in the program, and despite the challenges they faced they were all doing pretty well academically. It's a project that's very near and dear to Nerissa's heart, as she was in exactly the same situation when she first came to Cuthbertson at the age of fourteen. (Just to be clear, it happened well before I ever met her.)

"So the situation's resolved?"

She tossed her flowing tresses over her shoulders. "No, it's not the kind of situation that's gonna get a nice, tidy happy ending. Parker—that's the ex-boyfriend, you met him at that picnic last fall. Tall, blond, jock type."

"I remember him. He kept saying "bro" like he got paid for the use of the word. Also "dude." It got a bit grating."

"That's the one. He's not a bad guy, just a typical horny, self-obsessed teen."

"So you gave him a much-needed "Come to Jesus" lecture?"

"More like a gentle reminder that he has responsibilities. Anyway, enough about teens who are out of their depth. How about we get some yogurt?"

Once we were settled in our chairs again, Nerissa with a cup of pineapple-vanilla swirl with raspberries and strawberries, and me with a peppermint and fudge-brownie swirl with pecans, we resumed the conversation.

Nerissa was being extremely cautious not to spill yogurt on her clothing. "So, how are you feeling right now?"

I started with the blunt but accurate reply of "lousy," and once Nerissa shot me the universally used look that girlfriends give their boyfriends when they expect more than just a one-word response (they must learn it in fifth grade when they separate the kids by gender to teach them about their changing bodies), I went into more detail.

I'd told her the story many times. For me, it's one of those defining moments that you can't stop talking about, even when you'd rather not relive it. I didn't need to tell Nerissa again, but for the purposes of this narrative, I have to go back to one of the worst days of my life.

When I was in seventh grade, school was my refuge. My mother's second marriage was to a man who Satan kicked out of the innermost circles of hell for being too evil a bastard, even for the inferno's flames of the damned. My stepfather made most of my waking hours unendurable, except when I was safely away at Cuthbertson. Rough as it was for me, my younger half-brother had it even worse, in a very different way, thanks to my stepfather taking what I'll euphemistically call "an interest" in him, one that he didn't direct towards me. The walking, talking sack of excrement only directed verbal abuse in my direction. I didn't realize what was going on in the house until right before I moved in with my grandparents, and I was too wrapped up in my own preadolescent problems to notice what was going on right in front of me. At the time, I was on amiable but distant terms with most of my classmates. Bertie was my only close confidante.

Bertie, quite simply, was an awesome friend. He had a sixth sense for detecting when something was wrong, and finding a way to cheer you up completely. Whether it was stress over schoolwork, a soul-crushingly dismal home situation, or just the standard unpleasantness resulting from the unwanted onset of puberty, Bertie had a Midas touch for taking even the foulest mood and talking with you until he transfigured your feelings to the point where cartoon bluebirds started fluttering and chirping musically next to you.

Here's one of countless examples. One of our classmates, who I'll call Gillian, was being taunted by some our snottier peers. Now, a lesser fellow would have minded his own business and walked away, happy that the queen bee and her poisonous minions had directed their venom on some other unfortunate kid. Not Bertie. When he saw Gillian cornered on the playground, with the other girls bombarding her with the sort of barbs that leave most young women in similar situations with PTSD, Bertie marched right up to them, positioned himself between Gillian and the she-devils, and said, "Is this really the sort of people you want to be?" Well. You can bet the mortgage payment that the queen bee hadn't been asked that question before in her life. She tried to wound Bertie with a remark about his hair, but though her remark might have slashed most other kids like a razor, it drew no more blood from Bertie than a three-weeks-past-peak-ripeness peeled banana would have. Bertie just smiled, and started telling jokes and making silly faces. Pretty soon, the minions started chuckling, and despite her best efforts, pretty soon the queen bee was laughing, too, along with Gillian and myself.

That was just one of, according to my most conservative estimate, approximately eight billion times that Bertie stepped forward and turned a nasty or uncomfortable situation into something warm and friendly. Why did he make it his business to make school a better place for everybody? I have no idea. How did he develop his ability to make everything he touched brighter and kinder? Haven't a clue. Does it really matter? Bertie had a pure heart and the ability to make everybody he met his buddy. Every minute you spent talking with Bertie was a wonderful sixty seconds. He was, quite simply, a remarkable human being.

And then some monster murdered him.

It started out like any other early spring day. It was sunny, cool, and breezy. Nearly all the winter snow had melted by that point, aside from the remains of the massive piles at the edges of the parking lots. We all gathered in our homeroom classes, ready for another day of reading *A Raisin in the Sun* in English, studying South America in Geography, and mixing up polymers in Science, among other classroom pursuits. When I didn't see Bertie at the start of class, I assumed he was out with a cold. Then, after the Pledge of Allegiance, my homeroom teacher informed us that we were all heading into the Periodicals Room of the Middle School Library for an impromptu class meeting.

In retrospect, my memories of my walk from the classroom to the library are filled with foreboding and anxiety, but I'm pretty sure that I've been unconsciously embellishing my memories. In actuality, I believe that I expected nothing out of the ordinary, figuring that it was just some minor administrative declaration of little consequence to the students. All of the memories of dark premonitions are just after-the-fact embroideries. I know this because what happened next came as such an earth-shaking shock.

There were about seventy-five of us in our class at that time. We shuffled into the hard plastic chairs that had been set up, taking our seats in no particular order. This should have been a warning signal for me. I don't care for the connotations connected to the term "anal retentive," but I will grudgingly concede that Cuthbertson Hall loves to tell its students where to sit, whether it's in class, at lunch, or at assembly. When our teachers allowed us to sit wherever we wanted, I should have known that it was meant as a small comfort to soften the blow of something really terrible.

In the past, when the whole class was called together for an impromptu meeting, it usually meant that someone had done something wrong, but they didn't know who, so the whole class was being treated like suspects in the crime. This last happened a month earlier, when someone had sprayed shaving cream on a set of encyclopedias in the vice principal's office. We were all given little notecards and told to write down anything with knew about the vandalism. I knew nothing, but since no one identified the culprit, we were all forced to stay inside during recess for a week. As it turned out, the vice principal had started dating someone who was emotionally unstable, and it was this crazed love interest who had snuck into the school and sprayed the shaving cream after a bitter argument. It took a couple of weeks for this embarrassing news to trickle down to the student body, and when it did, we demanded apologies and an extra two and a half hours of recess. It wasn't until a couple of pushy parents took our side that we finally got something in the way of restitution in the form of an after-school pizza party.

When we were all called together for the shaving cream-coated encyclo-pedia incident, the faces of the teachers were stern and accusing. I knew something different and dreadful was afoot that fateful day when they all looked crushed, shaken, and a little scared. The Middle School guidance counselor marched to the front of the room with a solemn face, and by the time the first word was out of his mouth, my palms started sweating, and my intestines were tying themselves into square knots.

"Some of you may have heard this news already. For those of you that haven't, I'm afraid you're going to have to prepare yourself for a shock." He paused for what felt like a decade, and then he continued, explaining, "As you may have noticed, your classmate Bertie Godspeed is not here today. I have some terrible news for you. Bertie died yesterday afternoon...."

Years later, when I read Kurt Vonnegut's *Slaughterhouse-Five*, the opening line about coming "unstuck in time" jogged my memory. That's an excellent description of what happened at that moment. I became unstuck in time. Though my body was still firmly planted in a chair in the library, my mind was somewhere else, bouncing through memory after memory I had of Bertie, and sailing forward into scenes that I thought I'd have with Bertie in the years to come, like taking our dates to the prom and going on college trips, all significant life events in the future that Bertie would never experience. I was aware of the guidance counselor saying words like "shot while shopping at a neighborhood store," and "the police are investigating, but they haven't made any arrests yet," and "none of you are in any danger," but these phrases seemed to echo from a disembodied voice.

All I have in my memory are snippets of the rest of the day. I remember talking to various teachers. I know I cried the whole afternoon. I can't remember if I went to any classes or not. I know I went to lunch, but I'm pretty sure I didn't eat anything. I do remember when I finally came home, I was violently ill for a little while, and once I'd recovered, I retreated to the sanctuary of my room and dug out the board game Clue that I'd played with Bertie the last time he'd come over to hang out. I must have spent most of the rest of the evening pushing the playing pieces and weapons around the board, flipping cards over, and then turning them to their other sides again. I don't know why I did that. I just remember lacking the energy or inclination to do anything else.

My stepfather and half-brother left me alone that night, which was a blessing. My mother only said one thing to me that evening: "I'm sorry to hear about your friend." I'm pretty sure I skipped dinner that night, and I know for a fact that I didn't put on my pajamas and go to bed properly. When I woke up that morning, I was still wearing the previous day's school clothes and was lying on the rug. That pretty much set the tone for the next few days. Maybe other kids were similarly affected, but if they were, it escaped my notice.

While I'd given Nerissa the basic details of my reaction to the terrible news in the past, I'd never been especially specific. That afternoon, I described my memories so thoroughly that Marcel Proust himself would've rolled his eyes and groaned, saying, "Will you stop! We don't need to hear every single detail!" To her lasting credit, Nerissa listened without yawning, though after twenty minutes, she asked for a quick break and got up for seconds on the yogurt, though I noticed it was more berries than soft serve.

It's odd how some memories stay fuzzy and nebulous, no matter how much you focus on them, while others remain vivid and sharp, even if you spend your life trying to forget them. I remember the tie I was wearing that day (light blue with thin red stripes), the book I'd brought for free reading that day (an Erle Stanley Gardner Perry Mason mystery, *The Case of the Terrified Typist*). If I really strained my synapses, I could probably recall who was sitting where in the library for the announcement. Reliving these moments in high definition was having a bizarre effect on me. Every so often, I had the inexplicable sensation that I had somehow reverted to the seventh-grade version of my body and that a considerably shorter, much chubbier version of myself was now sitting in the chair. On occasion, I caught myself checking my coat to make sure that the sleeves hadn't suddenly become far too long and the waist much too narrow for me.

Yet try as I might, I simply could not remember delivering one of the eulogies at Bertie's funeral. I remember spending nearly all of my waking hours for two days writing and rewriting it. I distinctly recall walking up to the pulpit of the church, looking out at the pews that were crowded but not as jam-packed as I wished they'd be, and speaking, but try as I might, I can't recall one word of what I had to say. I could look it up. I know I still have the eulogy somewhere amongst several cubic yards of sealed plastic tubs filled with assorted files in a little storage space, but I can't bring myself to dig through them. Weird, isn't it, how one can't bring oneself to face certain memories, but simultaneously, one can't allow oneself to jettison the physical reminders of them forever, either?

That eulogy was a turning point for me on multiple levels. It was right before the funeral that I asked Mr. Godspeed to introduce me as "Funderburke" rather than "Isaiah." I knew I wasn't the same person I was just a few days earlier, and I wanted to separate myself from certain members of my supposed family as effectively as I could.

Returning to the present day, eventually, I ran out of fuel and had to stop talking. One can only reminisce about terrible times so much before one shuts down. "Thanks for listening to me," I muttered through dry lips.

"What are girlfriends for?" Nerissa shrugged. "I remember how you were the best buddy I could've hoped for our freshman year when my birth mother died."

At this point, it's necessary to provide some details into Nerissa's backstory. When she was fourteen, she scandalized a bunch of Concerned Parents™, when she showed up at Cuthbertson the summer before high school started with a chip on her shoulder and a newborn baby girl in a carrier. Nerissa's birth mom, who'd entered motherhood at about the same time in her life as Nerissa, was devoting all her energy to a losing battle with depression, and Nerissa's birth father had wanted nothing to do with her ever since her mother hadn't gotten the result she'd hoped for after urinating on a plastic stick. Realizing that her life wasn't heading in anywhere near the direction she wanted it to, Nerissa picked up her mother's credit card, bought a couple of plane tickets, and left her unhappy home in Los Angeles in favor of Milwaukee.

Why Milwaukee? Nerissa's Great-Aunt Scholastica is a legend at Cuthbertson, with a couple of hundred books published and nearly three-quarters of a century of teaching experience, and no plans to retire, despite being quite close to achieving her century. After her great-aunt proved sympathetic to her appeal, Nerissa was accepted into Cuthbertson, despite the protests of some Concerned Parents™ who were afraid she'd be a negative influence on their children. These fears proved unfounded, and aside from discovering and exploiting every possible loophole in Cuthbertson's dress code, Nerissa became a model student and kept her behavior completely G-rated from that point onwards.

Unfortunately, her personal life didn't go quite as smoothly as her academic career. Her birth mother died midway through her freshman year, and her future was in limbo until Keith Kaiming, then a novice history teacher who'd been recruited to help get Nerissa up to speed on the level of work expected of Cuthbertson students, was pressured and emotionally blackmailed into adopting her and the baby. The resulting father-daughter relationship turned out better than anyone could have hoped. Nerissa's GPA shot through the roof, Keith married a wonderful woman and made Nerissa a big sister multiple times over, and she went on to shine equally brightly in college and follow in her adoptive father's footsteps by pursuing a Ph.D. in American History, teaching at Cuthbertson, and mentoring other unwed teen mothers.

Nerissa kicked her right ankle over her left and stretched back in her chair. "Something else you should know. I talked to my parents, and they'd like to extend an invitation to the Godspeeds for dinner tomorrow. How does that sound to you?"

It was the best suggestion I'd heard all day, and I made my enthusiasm very clear to her. And so, a bit over twenty-four hours later, I arrived at the Kaiming house for Friday night dinner.

There are two words that invariably describe meals at the Kaimings: delicious and crowded. It makes sense when you have a huge extended family, and your fourteen-member household is largely spread out between two connected homes. Other than Keith and his wife Midge; there's Nerissa and her now-teenaged daughter Toby; both pairs of Keith and Midge's triplets; Keith's grandfather; and Midge's grandmother, sister, and brother. Keith's parents, who live about two miles away, also joined us, as did Mrs. Annenberg, the Kaimings' ninety-something neighbor who proudly lives by herself but hates eating alone. The Godspeed family, consisting of Bertie's parents and Zita, arrived right before I did. Not including myself, the final member of the dinner party was Mrs. Marigold Zwidecker, former teacher for both Bertie and myself, for both first and third grades, and also my landlady.

So with twenty-two chairs around a table with six leaves on it and so many plates and bowls of assorted foodstuffs that scarcely any of the tablecloth was visible, it had the makings of a smashing dinner with friends and family.

At least it would've been, if the whole atmosphere wasn't so uncomfortably awkward. When there's an elephant in the room, you can only ignore it for so long before it makes its presence known. We spent the first fifteen minutes munching and telling Midge and Keith how great the food was, and making mindless small talk, and it was increasingly clear with each passing second that none of us wanted to be the first to broach the topic on all of our minds.

Six-year-old Bernard is the eldest of Nerissa's little siblings, and though I'm not supposed to say such things, he's definitely my favorite. He's in Mrs. Zwidecker's class now, as she alternates two years teaching first grade and switches to two years teaching third, so some lucky kids get her twice. When Bernard looked up from his salmon cakes and demanded to know "What's going on? Why are all of you acting so weird?" it was a much-needed slap in the face to all of us. I started laughing, and most of the other adults at the table joined in with me. We stopped as soon as Bernard asked, "Does this have something to do with someone pretending to be Funderburke's dead friend?"

I broke the long silence. "Bernard, how did you know about that?"

"I was reading a book on a cushion behind a recliner yesterday when Nerissa came in and started talking on her phone. I wasn't eavesdropping, I just wanted to read quietly where my sisters wouldn't bother me." He shot a pointed look at the female two-thirds of the elder triplets, who responded in kind. "It's not my fault that Nerissa didn't bother to check behind the furniture or at least ask if anybody else was in the room. I would have told her I was there if she had. You were talking about someone named Bertie who died a while ago and someone bought credit cards in his name. Funderburke, are you going to catch the guy who killed him and stole his identity?"

I chuckled despite myself. "No. Remember how I told you that private detectives need to stay away from cases that the official police are investigating?"

"Yes, but you've said in the past that you can take that rule or leave it."

Making a mental note that I needed to be a lot more careful about what I said to Bernard in the future, I told him, "I was being facetious. Do you know what that means?"

"Does it mean you're saying you were kidding because you don't want me to know how serious you really were?"

Smart kid. "Yes. Yes, it does."

Bernard nodded triumphantly, clearly taking pride in being right. "So, who was Bertie, and how did he die?"

Midge cleared her throat. "Sweetie, what I have said before about discussing murders at the dinner table?"

"To wait until everybody's done eating," Bernard replied, looking chastened by the rebuke. To be fair to him, murders are a frequent topic of discussion in the Kaiming household, as Midge is a specialist in forensic medicine and criminal law, and has a pretty successful business as a consultant. She tries to keep her work away from her children, but I once caught Amara, her second-eldest biological daughter, using a butter knife to break into the file cabinet where Midge keeps graphic photos on two separate occasions, before I bought Midge some better locks.

Bernard had managed to break the ice, and the conversation proceeded a lot more naturally from that point forward. Everybody at the table broke into little groups and conversed. I was seated between Mr. and Mrs. Godspeed, and while homicide wasn't an appropriate conversation for the dinner table, there weren't any prohibitions against identity theft.

"Has there been any news?" I asked the Godspeeds.

"Nothing, I'm afraid," Mrs. Godspeed sighed.

"I called the police officers twice today," Mr. Godspeed added, "left some messages, but they didn't call back. To tell the truth, I don't think this is a top priority for them."

"I'm sure they're trying their best," his wife replied.

"Are they? The police "tried their best" nearly a decade and a half ago, and nothing came of it. And we can't call them slackers. They were smart men. Good men. Sharp detectives. They tried their best. And they failed. I'm not mad at them. Just disappointed. But someone took away my little boy and got away with it."

"He didn't get away with it," Mrs. Godspeed insisted. "We know what's happened to him. People who live lives like that don't make it this long. They overdose, or they get shot by another criminal, or they wind up in prison for something else. We're not going to know who he is, but I just know that one way or another, he's gotten his punishment." She stopped herself when she realized that Bernard was hanging on every word she was saying, and apologized to Keith and Midge. "You made it clear we weren't to discuss certain issues."

Keith smiled and waved a hand amiably. "You're our guests. You can talk about whatever you want."

And we did, but without coming right out and saying it, we decided that we weren't going to actually come out and talk about anything connected to Bertie. I described a couple of my more amusing recent investigations, and Mr. Godspeed talked about his work for a short while before realizing that his narrative wasn't very interesting and stopping in the middle of a story. Mrs. Zwidecker told us about the misadventures of some of her more mischievous students, and Bernard filled in a few additional details. It took a while, but the tone of the evening became pleasant and relaxing, which is exactly what the Godspeeds and I needed.

After we'd all had our fill, and there were still enough leftovers on the table to keep the Kaimings well-nourished for the remainder of the weekend, Zita and Toby retreated to one corner of the house, presumably to talk about girl stuff. The Kaiming kids took their desserts with them and left to play quietly, and the adults settled into the living room for homemade chocolate pound cake.

I caught Mrs. Godspeed's eye, and through an unspoken agreement, we both decided that we were sick of small talk.

"So, I suppose you're all wondering about Bernard's identity being stolen." For the benefit of those who weren't aware of what had happened, Mrs. Godspeed summarized the events of two nights earlier, condensing it into three minutes. At the end she sighed, and declared, "Unfortunately, the police think that this was one of those scams where the criminals take as much as they can all in one go, and then abandon the credit cards. They're probably pretty experienced with these things, and they know how to keep themselves from getting caught."

"And I say the police are wrong." Mr. Godspeed spoke quietly, but with such force he made everybody flinch a bit.

"Why do you say that, Mr. Godspeed?" Nerissa asked.

"Because I've been thinking about it, and the police didn't ask the right questions. They asked if we'd thrown out any important papers. They asked if anybody had been asking questions about Bertie. But I started doing some research on the Internet, and it made me think. How did they know Bertie's birth date? I ran some searches. I couldn't find it anywhere. He died in the mid-1990s, long before everything got posted online. And his full birthday isn't on his tombstone. Just his birth year. How did they get that information?"

I thought about it a moment. "Most of the major libraries have the Milwaukee newspapers on microfilm. Someone could have been digging through those obituaries. And some police files are on Internet databases, if you know where to look and can get access."

"But what about his Social Security Number?" Mr. Godspeed asked. "That wasn't in his obituary."

"Could someone have broken into Cuthbertson's old files and found Bertie's information?" Nerissa theorized.

"I doubt it," I replied. "Cuthbertson only got the Internet in 1995, a bit after Bertie was killed. All the old digitized information is on hard drives and servers with no online access. Part of my security work makes sure that all the old records are securely under lock and key. The only people who could gain access to that are…." A knot formed in my gut, and I felt my palms start to sweat. "Cuthbertson employees." I tried to dismiss the thought that it was an inside job at the school. "What about Bertie's personal papers? Where do you keep them?"

"In a safe at home. We haven't taken them out in years," Mr. Godspeed answered.

Mrs. Godspeed stirred. "That's not exactly true. I took out the file with Bertie's birth certificate and Social Security card a couple of months ago for a meeting for Bertie's Buddies. I didn't need the personal information, I wanted to put some of the photos on the website. You know I have trouble looking at old photos because the memories get overwhelming, but there was a baby picture in the folder I just had to see. I left the file on the table. I suppose someone could've looked through it at one point, but why would they do that? They're not criminals."

"Did you put the file away in the safe?" I asked.

"Right after the meeting."

"Who was there?"

"I don't remember. Not all the members of the Board of Directors were there. Only about four of them. I'd have to ask Esme. She keeps the minutes." Esme was Mrs. Godspeed's assistant, a longtime volunteer.

Mr. Godspeed put down his empty cake plate and leaned forward. "Isaiah, I know this is a lot to ask, but would you consider looking into this? I know it's an open police investigation, but...."

"Exactly. I can't interfere with an open investigation...." A loophole popped into my head. "But I now have reason to suspect that Cuthbertson security may have been breached. It's certainly a possibility. That is my job. I'm totally justified in looking into that, and if I find anything connected to Bertie getting ghosted, I'll be happy to pass on the information to the police. That makes my digging around okay At least, okay-ish."

Mr. Godspeed smiled a tight little grin. "Thank you, Isaiah. We'll pay you–"

"The hell you will." There was no anger in my voice, only firmness.

We talked for another three-quarters of an hour, and then it was time for the youngest Kaiming kids to go to bed, which seemed like a reasonable time to break up the party.

Before we left, Toby came up to me. "Thanks for the book recommendations." She's into supernatural suspense and horror, and I told her to check out some novels by John Bellairs from the Middle School Library. He was one of my favorite authors growing up, and Toby and I discussed his work for a few minutes. She also brought up the fact that she was having trouble with a snotty young woman who was making unpleasant comments about Nerissa and her past, so I gave Toby some tips on how to defuse the situation without violence.

As I started to drive Mrs. Zwidecker back home, she studied my face for a bit and sighed. "What are you thinking about, Mrs. Z?"

"I was reflecting on the fact that I think you're too close to this case, Isaiah. I know you've never completely given up on your dream of solving Bertie's murder, and I know how you get obsessed with righting injustices."

"Are you telling me not to take the case?"

"I'm telling you not to let it consume your life. And you also need to be prepared for what happens if you find out who stole Bertie's identity. What are you going to do if you come face to face with the person who pretended to be him? How will you respond if you find out who actually killed him?"

I'd been asking myself what would happen if I ever met Bertie's killer for over half my life. The answers I told myself frightened me.

Chapter Three

Do You Realize You Were Screaming?

I'm a heavy sleeper. Abnormally so. Once my eyelids shut for the night, you could tie strings to the top and bottom halves of my eyelashes, set me down on a railroad track, and attach the strings to a pair of trains headed in opposite directions at full speed, and even then you couldn't get my eyes to open. It's always been this way for me. As an adolescent, I wasn't at my best unless I managed to hit the sack for a full twelve hours, which was only feasible on weekends due to the gargantuan Cuthbertson Hall homework load. Even today, I require nine to ten solid hours of blissful unconsciousness if I'm going to bring my "A" game, and when I need to be up for work, I have five alarms going—a small digital travel clock, a clock radio set to a station that plays techno music (which I hate), a black hard plastic clock with the voice of Stephen Fry in character as Jeeves which provides dry and polite awakening messages, a spherical glass bulb designed to glow steadily brighter over the course of ten minutes, and a brass wind-up clock the size of a dinner plate which I keep ten feet away from the other alarms, so I have to actually get out of bed to silence it. I've never actually tried this experiment, but if I were to take that brass wind-up clock down to the city morgue, I'm pretty sure it could wake the dead with—at minimum—a fifty percent success rate. A while back, Nerissa gave me a little clock that's supposed to squirt you with ice water, but I toss and turn a lot and throw the covers over my head as I sleep, so the spray missed me most of the time, and it nearly damaged some books I had on my end table. And even with all of these awakening devices at my disposal, Mrs. Zwidecker still has to let herself into my little house to shake me awake at least once a week, so I'm not late for work.

Mrs. Marigold Zwidecker and I have been close ever since she was my first-grade teacher. My contempt for inferior educators is matched only by my admiration for great ones, and Mrs. Zwidecker is not just a scholastic gem, she's the whole darn Crown Jewels. She can manage to make the first and third-grade curricula fascinating, devise all sorts of enjoyable hands-on classroom activities, and handle troublemakers and bullies like a boss. Not only did she give me two of the best academic years of my life, but I firmly believe that I would never have survived my parents' interminable divorce without her support. We remained in touch throughout Middle School, Upper School, and college, and afterwards, when I needed a place to live, and a recently widowed Mrs. Zwidecker had an empty guest cottage in a corner of her backyard, we became tenant and landlady, which proved to be a mutually beneficial arrangement, as she often needs help with maintaining her house and grounds, and she loves to be able to cook for somebody.

Normally when I'm awakened by Mrs. Zwidecker's hands shaking my shoulders, I become aware of all of the alarm clocks going off around me. This time, however, the room was silent, and there was no trace of sunlight filtering in from behind the curtains.

"Mrs. Zwidecker? What time is it? What day is it?"

"It's Saturday, and it's just after two in the morning."

"What? Did my brass alarm clock go off?" Normally, when the brass alarm rings for more than thirty seconds or so, Mrs. Zwidecker can hear it from her house, and she knows she needs to let herself into my dwelling in order to awaken me.

"No. Do you realize you were screaming?"

"Was I? Are you sure?"

"Ask anybody within a quarter-mile. They heard you. You were dreaming about poor Bertie."

"How do you know that?"

"I heard you calling out at the top of your lungs, "Don't shoot Bertie! Don't hurt him!" Over and over and over again, getting louder every time."

It took a few more moments, but I gradually regained my memories of the nightmare I'd been having right before Mrs. Zwidecker shook me out of it. My subconscious had been piling up all of the memories I'd been having about Bertie lately, and how exactly my brain had managed to get David Lynch to direct my horrible dream, I'll never know, but the long and the short of it was that I was twelve years old again, standing in a corner of the shop where Bertie was killed (even though I'd never actually seen it other than in photographs and on that grainy video). I was unable to move, forced to watch this monstrous dark figure composed of oozing slime and wafting shadow, as it aimed a gun at Bertie, fired, and slithered away as Bertie fell to the ground. I screamed the entire time, and the process repeated over and over again, somehow becoming more frightening and increasingly surreal every time.

It felt like the nightmare had lasted for several hours, but it must have been considerably less than that. I have pretty powerful lungs, but I must have been bellowing at full volume if it was enough for Mrs. Zwidecker to wake up after hearing me from inside her house.

"Do you need to talk about it? I've been thinking about Bertie a lot lately, too, as you know."

Good old Mrs. Zwidecker. (I shouldn't use the word "old." She wouldn't care for that.) I wanted to talk with her, but I realized that she needed her sleep, and I informed her of both of these facts. After assuring her that she didn't need to get me anything, I thanked her, and after locking the door as she left, I poured myself a glass of water and sat in my most comfortable chair in the dark as I attempted to screw my head back on straight and get my heart rate back under a hundred and fifty beats per minute before returning to bed.

As is often the case when I wake up in the middle of the night disoriented and barely functional, I found my slowly settling mind turning to unpleasant memories. I mentally replayed that awful afternoon in the back of the Middle School Library over and over, listening to the somber announcement about

Bertie.

I'd thought about that wretched memory constantly over the years, but this was one of the rare times I allowed myself to reflect upon the broader implications of that day. When my parents divorced, my happy, innocent childhood years were finished, but I was still a little kid. Bertie's death marked the end of childhood, or more accurately, the slow death of childhood. Childhood doesn't just wrap up neatly at a set time, like how at the stroke of midnight on December thirty-first, one year ends forever and another begins. I don't think there's a cutoff point separating childhood and adolescence, like your thirteenth birthday or the sudden appearance of your first pimple or anything like that. I think that it's a more gradual shift over months, maybe over a year, as the era of childhood slowly fades away and is gradually yet inexorably replaced by the hormone-infused, angst-addled age we euphemistically dub adolescence.

Because I know that before I walked into the library for that unexpected assembly in the spring of seventh grade, I was still a child. The day I started high school, I had completely metamorphosed into an adolescent. But in-between...I don't think it was a steady evolution. It just happened without my realizing it. If you'd asked me at any point during eighth grade, I would have insisted that I was still firmly in the prime of my childhood. It's only through hindsight that I'm able to detect the dramatic changes happening to me during that time, physically, mentally, and spiritually.

Physically, I somehow managed to be pretty clueless as to what was happening to me until the changes were too dramatic to overlook. Ever since the divorce, I sought out comfort wherever I could get it, and food, consisting of as many helpings at meals as I could cram into my mouth and plenty of sweets as needed, was the most reliable way to generate a little brightness to break up the misery. I admit that I never came close to losing my baby fat as a kid, but after over four years of turning to cookies to help me make it from one day to the next, I was nearly as wide as I was tall. I am probably exaggerating, but that's how I picture myself in my mind. Grandma was a great baker, and when I came over to her house to visit, she was always in the kitchen making treats. I think she realized two things.

The first was that it wasn't healthy for me to try to eat my way out of my messed-up divorce-inflicted emotions. The second was that nothing else was working at all, and if the price of a few all-too-brief respites from the PTSD of family court meant some extra inches to my waistline, well, it wasn't an ideal solution, but it was better than nothing. Grandma knew that she couldn't get the man I'd thought was my father to love me again, nor could she force my mother to find a comfortable place for me in her new family, but she could produce a crumb cake every now and then as a temporary means of consolation.

So by the time of Bertie's death, my potbelly was dramatically distended. The timing certainly was coincidental, but my first major growth spurt probably started sometime around March of seventh grade, maybe a bit earlier or later. At that time, I started growing taller at the rate of nearly half an inch a month, a process lasting the better part of a year. About a week after hearing the news about Bertie, I started getting my first growing pains.

To this day, whenever I hear the phrase, "whatever doesn't kill you makes you stronger," I feel the urge to respond to whoever parroted that stupid cliché by chucking a moldy tomato at the idiotic speaker's face. Even if you survive something that endangers your life and sanity, it's more likely than not you'll be left weakened and scarred, potentially permanently. As long as I'm ranting about things that tick me off, I want to sound off on those treacly videos that we were forced to watch in the fifth grade, telling us what a wondrous and exciting time we were entering with the advent of puberty.

What a crock. If the people writing the moronic scripts to those videos had a quarter-ounce of honesty and insight between them, they would've done far better to come right out and tell us, "Puberty is a very special time in your life when your own body is trying to kill you. If a pharmaceutical company were to take the chemicals that are about to start being pumped through your bodies and brains, and dump them into your drinking water, you could successfully sue them for hundreds of billions of dollars. It's not gonna be fun, and between your emotions and physical discomfort, not to mention the whole social awkwardness that comes from being surrounded by scores of young people going through exactly what you are, half the time

35

you'll convince yourself that you're not going to make it through puberty alive. But the odds are overwhelmingly in your favor that you will, and after your body and mind finally stop going cuckoo on you, you'll realize that you survived, just in time to move on to a whole new set of challenges that come with adulthood. Yay. Bottom line, there's no cure and there's no anesthetic for what you're going through. The only option is to fasten your seatbelt and ride it out, but at least you can take cold comfort in knowing that you're surrounded by other people going through their own version of what you're enduring."

I tell this to students who are having a tough time with adolescence as part of my policy to only use brutally honest straight talk. I'm told it helps. It isn't very comforting, but it's nice to get a reminder that this, too, shall pass.

The only good thing about puberty is that you can tell yourself you're developing and growing up and becoming an adult. In a few more decades, maybe a lot less, you have to deal with the aches and pains of arthritis, worn-out joints, sore backs, and a myriad of other discomforts that are part and parcel of aging. That's an inevitable decline leading to taking your seat in God's waiting room. At least with puberty, you can tell yourself that you're coming up to the start of your independent adult life. You put up with physical discomfort and psychological angst your whole life. But when you're a teenager, you've never been through anything quite that awful before, so it looms in your psyche and overshadows the later low points in your life.

End of rant. Back to my reminiscing about the hellish torture that was growing pains.

The spring of seventh grade is when I started feeling like each of my limbs was being twisted off by an invisible giant who was using me as a stress relief doll. The sharp stabbing sensations, the dull throbbing soreness, and similar other forms of agony would afflict me at all sorts of inopportune times, often when I was sleeping or trying to sleep. The pain wasn't all day, every day, but it was frequent enough to be a constant, distracting presence in my life. The last couple of months of seventh grade are mostly a blur to me, with my primary memories being my wondering why Bertie's killer hadn't been arrested yet, and enduring my growing pains. Somehow, I still managed to do pretty well in all of my classes, but I don't see how I kept my place on the honor roll. I must have learned a lot during that time, but I was lost in my own mind, focused on my grief, pain, and sense of injustice.

Starting in early April, I started getting severe stomach cramps and dry mouth. I'd find it difficult to eat more than a few bites at a time, as the food would seem to expand in my mouth the more I chewed it. Most days, I was surviving mainly on milk and juice because I could barely consume any solid food. Then, after three or four days of a liquid diet, the situation would reverse, and I'd suddenly become voraciously hungry, to the point that I'd wolf down everything in the house that was even remotely edible. Grandma, who equated food with love, worried about me, but my pediatrician assured her that this happened to some kids during puberty, and prescribed me plenty of nutritious soft foods, and also suggested some smoothie recipes. Some of the smoothies were fine, but the broccoli and cauliflower blend made me feel even worse.

How much of this was some sort of psychological fallout from the murder, and how much was physiological from puberty, I'll never know. And I don't care to explore the topic— it's not a time in my life I enjoy reliving. The situation continued through the end of the school year, and through the summer. I found myself full of nervous energy, and when my grandparents went to the community pool for water exercises, I joined them and burned off my emotional tumult through swimming countless laps.

It's probably not surprising that everything I mentioned took its toll on my body. My observational skills have always been first-rate, but because I was stuck in my own messed-up, puberty-shadowed world, I didn't notice the gradual changes. My grandparents must have made some comments along the way, but they didn't register. During the summer, I wore almost solely T-shirts and cotton shorts, and though I remember frequently adjusting the drawstrings, I didn't make the connection between tightening the waistband and what was going on with me. All I know is that shortly before school started again in the fall, I tried on my uniform from the previous year to see if it still fit. It didn't.

As I gaped at my reflection in my full-length mirror, I saw that my clothes were both too large and too small. The cuffs of my trousers fell so high above my feet they were practically capri pants. The sleeves of my dress shirt didn't come close to my wrists. But the shirt billowed around my frame, and as I held out the waistband of my pants, I realized that there was more than enough room for two of the current version of me in them. I stared at myself in my ill-fitting garments for a little while, pulled off the shirt and let the pants fall to my ankles, and for the first time, realized that physically, I had transformed completely from the medium-height, stocky kid of six months earlier, without my realizing it. I was considerably taller, and I didn't recognize my own face. My round cheeks had completely deflated, my double chin had vanished, and my cheekbones were now clearly discernable. My formerly thick limbs were now like twigs. As for my torso... The boy bosoms that had long been the subject of much teasing by bullies in the gym locker room were gone without a trace, and the faint outlines of some of my ribs were just barely discernible. Most notably, my belly, which had always been soft and round as long as I could remember, and which had protruded steadily further with each passing year, had evaporated as well. The place where my paunch used to be was as firm and flat as a wooden board. I tried to squeeze my sides, expecting to fill my hands with thick folds of flesh, but instead, my fingers could grasp only little pinches of skin.

I was stunned. I had always identified as a fat kid, and I was fine with it. It was a part of my identity, and I felt like I had been transplanted into someone else's body as I whispered, "Oh...my...gosh...I'M SKINNY!!!"

In the popular imagination, there's a widespread belief that when an overweight kid slims down dramatically; a sudden surge of confidence, happiness, popularity, and attractiveness to the opposite gender results, and a reinvention of one's self-image follows as well. Maybe that's happened to other young people who've been through that sort of transformation, but for me, the biggest change that happened to me was that I had to radically resize my wardrobe, which was no picnic for my unfortunate grandmother, who had to endure my whining, because I hate shopping for anything that isn't either food or books, and I never enter a clothing store if I can possibly help it. In any case, my general attitude was marred by stereotypical teenage emo brattiness at that point.

As I entered eighth grade, slim and sullen, I was fully aware I was a very different person from the boy I was just six months earlier, and I would have given fifty years of my life to be magically transformed back into the shell-shocked-by-divorce kid who carried the evidence of eating his feelings on his waistline, and who was gradually teaching himself how to be happy and start trusting people again. Now I was bitter and angry, mostly due to the fact that Bertie's murder case was still unsolved, but also because the evil puberty chemicals were warping my brain and turning me into a real pill, and because my scrawny body was terribly battered. When you shed a lot of pounds really fast, the phenomenon of "phantom fat" means that you keep allowing extra room for your posterior when you sit, so when you descend on a chair with that radically shrunken portion of your anatomy, you often stop lowering yourself a couple of inches above the seat, and your center of gravity's off, so you frequently bruise your tailbone and sometimes even slide off the chair, much to the amusement of your peers.

I firmly believe in nonviolence except in life-threatening emergencies, but if I were to come across the emaciated little snot that I was in September of eighth grade, I'd punch younger me straight on the jaw, knocking teenage me to the ground, and I'd stand over adolescent Funderburke and say, "Trust me, you deserve that." Because, at that time, I was not channeling my anger and frustration in a healthy manner. I was snapping at anybody who approached me. When my seventh-grade math teacher, Mrs. Liddens, stopped me in the hall and commented on how thin I was, I glowered at her and snarled, "I have tapeworms," and stomped away. She didn't deserve that, and I apologized to her profusely a few weeks later after my come to Jesus moment at my intervention.

I don't want to record all of my unpleasant attitudes and snide remarks over the course of September of eighth grade. In my defense, a lot of other teens have acted a heck of a lot worse during adolescence, but that doesn't excuse my general vileness. I can see what a stinking turd I was with the benefit of hindsight, but at the time, I had total tunnel vision and couldn't see my own orneriness. So I was confused and defensive on the last Friday afternoon of September, when Grandma drove me home from school, and I entered the living room. I expected to see Grandpa sitting in his chair, watching television. But the T.V. was off, and not only was Grandpa seated in the living room, but so were Mrs. Zwidecker; my uncle, Fr. Francis Funderburke; and Mr. and Mrs. Godspeed. Grandma lowered herself onto the loveseat, the last remaining place to sit, and gestured to me to join her.

I don't have to recount exactly what was said. I'm fairly certain that most people will be able to fill in the details themselves. I immediately asked what was going on, and after a chorus of voices telling me how much I was loved and cared about, the members of my family and the guests, who were as good as family to me, started to talk about how worried they were about me and how concerned they were about how angry I'd been lately.

I pointed out that I'd been angry for five years, ever since the divorce. Uncle Francis pointed out, quite rightly, that this was a different kind of anger, and they suspected that it had something to do with Bertie's murder.

Jumping to my feet, I ranted for quite some time about how I had a right to be angry. It'd been half a year, and Bertie's killer still hadn't been arrested yet. What was wrong with the police? I remember every word I shouted, but I'm not going to write them down. Just thinking about it is making the white-hot rage smolder in me again, and right now, it's not going to do me any good to bring back the old memories and emotions. Funny, one would think that they'd fade over time, but I've been discovering that instead of blurring in my mind, the worst events of the past and all of the powerful feelings they evoked in me are only growing more intense with time, and just remembering them is enough not only to reopen an old wound, but to create a couple of new wounds as well. The recollection of past anger is like a bunch of shards of broken glass tossed onto a lake. In many cases, the water currents and shifting sand wear away the sharp edges of the glass until the fragments are smooth and incapable of causing harm. But sometimes, the glass isn't dulled and remains sharp, lying in wait for some unwary wader to walk in the water, only to recoil in horror at the sensation of a stab wound in the sole of his foot, and the unnerving sight of a faint feathery plume of his own blood drifting up towards the surface of the water.

My ranting at my loved ones lasted for more than five minutes, probably closer to ten. After bursting a few dozen blood vessels, my mouth finally was rendered dry to the point of rendering me silent, and my tirade was thankfully brought to a much-needed halt. I fell backwards onto the loveseat, shooting a death glare around the room at the only people in the world who really cared about me. After a few moments, silent save for the sound of my own pulse radiating through a vein in my head, Uncle Francis leaned forward and quietly but clearly asked, "Isaiah, do you think that Bertie, may his soul rest in peace, would want you to feel this angry for so long?"

That struck a nerve. I'd never thought of how Bertie would want me to deal with the emotional fallout of his murder before that moment, and I think my bewilderment was clear to everybody else.

"You know he wouldn't," Mrs. Godspeed reminded me.

"Knowing that he couldn't bear to let us live our lives in anger is what's given me the power to move beyond my own frustrations," Mr. Godspeed added.

I started to say something, failed, tried again, and similarly came up empty. And then the miracle happened. I hadn't cried since I heard the news about Bertie. I'd raged, I'd fumed, I'd sulked, I'd punched my pillow while trying and failing to sleep at night. But I hadn't managed to generate tears. Not one. And now, over half a year delayed, I was doing my best impression of Niagara Falls.

This lasted for over an hour. Grandma pressed tissue after tissue into my shaking hands, and by the time I'd depleted the entire box, I was dangerously in need of being rushed to the emergency room due to dehydration. Mrs. Zwidecker left the room and returned with a glass of water for me, and after thanking her and draining it in a massive gulp, I finally had enough command of my vocal cords to ask my loved ones, "So…what should I do now?"

Back in the present, I asked myself that question again and again, sitting in my chair in the dark, and coming up with no new answers or even coherent thoughts, just old memories and emotions that seemed more tangible than any of my possessions scattered around the room. I'm not sure when I fell asleep again, but I was eventually awakened by pounding at my door. It took the strength of Hercules and Atlas combined, but I managed to rise out of my beloved chair and to the door, to find Nerissa standing there.

"You look even worse than on Thursday," she informed me.

I wanted to reply with something barbed and memorable, but not only was Nerissa looking amazing in a way that would melt men tougher than me into slobbering piles of testosterone and drool, but from the way I felt, I knew she was right.

"What time is it?"

"Three-thirty," she replied. "Did you just wake up?"

"Yeah. I had a rough night."

"Mrs. Zwidecker told me you were screaming at two this morning. She said that one of the neighbors called her to complain just as she was leaving the house to wake you."

"Yeah, I have great lungs. You know I don't smoke."

"Are you okay? Are you going to be able to come to Mass with me?"

"Of course. Give me six and a half minutes." I could be precise because I'd done this before, thanks to my long habit of oversleeping and rushing to get ready in the morning. Or, in this case, late afternoon. It was too close to Mass to eat, so that saved precious moments. I performed the necessary washing, brushing, shaving, and dressing in record time, and by the time I slipped into a suit and my walking coat, I'd only needed six minutes and twelve seconds, as Nerissa, who'd been timing me with the stopwatch app on her phone, informed me in a tone that was sufficiently good-natured to assure me that she hadn't acted out of impatience.

Mrs. Zwidecker joined us in Nerissa's candy apple-red sports car, and we all made it to Sts. Crispin and Crispinian's On-the-Lake in the nick of time. After Mass ended, Keith and Midge attempted to herd their kids into the minivan, succeeding in five out of six cases. Their second-oldest biological daughter, Amara, insisted on playing tag with a bunch of other children who were releasing their pent-up energy by running around in circles. I excused myself, and went to talk to my uncle.

I stood off to the side, waiting for the remaining parishioners to finish talking to Uncle Francis. It took rather longer than I'd hoped, as a couple of elderly women in line insisted on chatting. They struck me as the lonely sort who live alone, and going to church is their sole social engagement of the week, so I understood why they seized every chance they had for blathering, even if my patience was starting to wear thin.

Uncle Francis saw me, and did his best to keep the line moving. Once everybody was on their respective ways, he motioned me back inside the church, and we sat next to each other in the back pew.

"I heard about your friend, Isaiah."

"Do you know all the details?"

"About the identity theft? The basics. I'm more concerned about what how you're doing."

"Emotionally, physically, or spiritually?"

"All of the above."

I nodded. "Physically, I haven't been sleeping well, so there's that. I have a nasty knot in my gut that's not getting any better. Emotionally, things are pretty worked up. Spiritually? You know how there's one thing that no matter how hard I try, I can never really succeed at doing. Forgiveness."

"That's a common problem with people."

"It's not like I don't try. I try forgiving people, and it works for a while. Then a week, a month later, I start thinking about what they did. I don't do it on purpose, but all the old anger comes back, usually worse than before."

"That's a common problem. It's a mistake to think that you just have to say the words "I forgive you" and all the anger and resentment disappears forever. You have to keep trying. It's like quitting smoking. You have to keep trying until one attempt finally succeeds. And if you backslide, you get back on the horse as soon as you can. It's not easy, but it's worth it. Even if you have to do it seventy times seven times, four hundred ninety times."

"I guess…."

"Who specifically are you thinking of that you're having difficulty forgiving, Isaiah?"

"A bunch of people. Bertie's killer, for one."

"It's difficult to forgive someone you don't actually know. It's one thing to talk to someone who's wronged you, realize that they're a fallible human being, and understand why they did what they did. It's harder to forgive an abstraction."

"That's exactly what Bertie's killer is to me. He has no face, but he's a monster. He's an enormous, shadowy figure, not made out of flesh and blood, but smoke and ooze. Of course, he was just an average human being. At least on the outside."

"Do you believe that on the inside, Bertie's murderer was something terrible?"

"Sometimes. Maybe his killer was some sociopath with no sense of right and wrong. Perhaps he was a sadist who took pleasure in causing pain. More likely, he was an addict who was so strung out he didn't know what he was doing. But what really scares me is the fact that he totally got away with it. What happens to someone who gets away with murder? I don't know from experience, but my gut tells me that if the killer isn't crippled by guilt, then he starts thinking that he's invincible, that he can commit the worst possible crimes without penalty. How can that not go to your head?"

"I spoke to the Godspeeds a couple of years ago. They told me that they'd made their peace with not knowing the killer's identity, as the police assured them that they already knew his fate based on statistics."

"Right. Dead from gang violence or an overdose or rotting in prison for another crime. And even if he escapes earthly justice, he'll get divine justice."

"Isaiah, what have I told you about wishing for people to burn in hell for eternity?"

"To stop doing it."

"Exactly."

"I just can't stop feeling that sometimes divine mercy seems like an opportunity for the worst people in the world to beat the system."

"It's not "beating the system," Isaiah, it's setting things right. Justice is more than punishment. True justice involves the sinner's soul getting purified."

"Am I wrong to want punishment?"

"It's natural and understandable. You have a very strong sense of right and wrong. That's a blessing. But it can harm you as well, for when you see something you consider an injustice, you become obsessed, and you wind up hurting yourself while the person who committed the injustice isn't affected at all by the rage that burns you up on the inside."

"Do you think I should try to let things go?"

"Letting go is a level of advice on par with taking two aspirin. It's a common solution to problems, but it only helps with a handful of troubles. It does no good to let go of things that are made to stick with us, and the desire for justice is an important part of who you are. But does letting thoughts of punishing Bertie's killer consume you make you a better person?"

"Uncle Francis, Patricia Highsmith once declared that "I find the public passion for justice quite boring and artificial, for neither life nor nature cares if justice is ever done or not." But that's not true. Think about how the Godspeeds' lives were damaged by not knowing the truth. I think that life *does* care if justice is done, because terrible crimes wound your soul and psyche, and any attempt to make the situation heal without addressing the central issue head on—who committed the atrocity and how are they going to atone for it—is bound to fail. And as for nature... Well, *I* am a force of nature, and I care about justice being done."

Uncle Francis chuckled softly. "You have always been passionate about seeing wrongdoers get their comeuppance. Which makes me wonder, how are you coming with forgiving your family members?"

I ran my toe over the pew kneeler. "Well, I don't bear my biological father any grudges. I don't know who or where he is, nor does my mother, and more likely than not, he doesn't know about my existence, so I'm not going to hold a grudge against him. He was just a common fornicator who didn't act with malice. So what the heck. Whoever he is, he and I are good. The guy I thought was my father the first eight years of my life? You know what he said to me."

"Yes, that was unbelievably cruel."

"He hasn't spoken to me directly in a decade and a half, and the last I heard of him was shortly after I turned eighteen when his lawyer threatened me with a restraining order if I wrote or called him again. I get why he hates me. I'm the cuckoo in the nest. A constant reminder that he wasn't enough for his woman. I'm done with him. I don't hate him anymore, I just pity him. A man who can bear so much rancor for a little kid deserves sympathy."

"But there's still some anger there."

"I'm working on it. Not succeeding very well, but I believe that Jesus gives points for effort."

"And your mother? And half-brother?"

"As far as I'm concerned—" I was interrupted by the parish secretary bursting into the church.

"Excuse me, Father, but there's a call for you. You're needed at the hospital for Last Rites."

Uncle Francis rose from the pew. "I apologize for cutting this short—"

"Don't worry about it. You're doing the Lord's work. Go and make sure a soul goes straight to Heaven."

We walked out to the parking lot together, and I rejoined Nerissa and Mrs. Zwidecker.

"Feeling better, Funderburke?"

"Better-ish. It's a step in the right direction." The fact that I hadn't eaten all day was starting to take its toll on me, and I fished a chocolate mint protein bar out of a coat pocket.

"I just got a call from Mrs. Godspeed. She's been thinking about it, and she believes she's got a list of the people who could have gotten Bertie's Social Security Number and other information." Nerissa smiled. "I'm guessing you want to go and check out the suspects?"

I matched her grin with a bigger one of my own. "Bet on it!"

Chapter Four

God Is Not Your Butler

We dropped Mrs. Zwidecker off at home and made our way across town to the headquarters of Bertie's Buddies. I've tried to look up the statistics for how long the average nonprofit lasts, but the Internet provides conflicting answers. Some websites say a third of all nonprofits are dissolved within a few years of being created; others put the percentage at half or even seventy percent. Whatever the true number is, I'm pretty sure that the odds against a nonprofit surviving past its fifth birthday are pretty high. Bertie's Buddies made it to its tenth anniversary. That's a triumph.

Bertie's Buddies is all about helping kids. It takes a two-pronged approach to the problems facing young people. Their volunteers go to schools, delivering presentations, performing skits, showing movies, and reading books to the littlest kids. It's all part of an effort to educate kids on how to treat each other better, notice when a pal is in trouble, and get help when necessary. I like to think of it as child empowerment. Kids have a deep-seated desire to help others, but sometimes they don't know the right strategies to assist their friends in certain situations. Simultaneously, Bertie's Buddies leads benevolent efforts to keep children in need fed and clothed, and even sheltered if possible. Bertie's Buddies often works in tandem with other Milwaukee charities, so if they can't help some kid in need, they try to find another charity or nonprofit that can.

Most charities named for a murdered kid would have a photograph of that child prominently displayed on all promotional materials, but Mrs. Godspeed had long ago vetoed any use of Bertie's image. Seeing his face emblazoned everywhere would have been too painful for her.

The big question is "How many young people has this helped?" It's impossible to tell. Mrs. Godspeed tells me they've gotten over fifteen hundred letters from kids over the years telling them how Bertie's Buddies has helped them through tough situations and a handful of angry messages informing the volunteers that their stupid advice has ruined their lives. Last year, Mr. Godspeed showed me some of the hate mail, asking me to look into it, as he worried that the writers might come after Mrs. Godspeed or even Zita, seeking revenge. All sixteen angry letters were anonymous, but I noticed that even though they were written with different pens on mostly different pieces of paper, the envelopes were identical, and the stamps were all the same style. Plus, the writer tried to alter his handwriting, but even though I only have a basic knowledge of graphology, I discerned a bunch of similarities in the lettering. A reference to a specific school and presentation narrowed down the suspects to a seventh-grade class of ninety-four, and after my failed attempt to charm their English teacher into showing me their handwritten book reports failed, I had better luck with their science teacher. Until Nerissa, I had extremely limited success with women my own age, but there is one segment of the female population that always has taken a liking to me: highly educated women in their more mature years. If someone were to ask me to name an Oscar-winning actress who I would hit it off best with, I would unhesitatingly say Ruth Gordon. Assuming she even remotely resembled her character in *Harold and Maude*, and she was still alive, the two of us would get along like gangbusters. In any event, the science teacher allowed me to look at her class's science reports, and I was able to recognize not just one student's handwriting, but the fact that he'd made the same spelling errors in the letters as well. After being confronted, the kid gleefully confessed, declared it was all a prank, and cast aspersions on my career choices. I got my own back when I informed his mother of what her son had been doing, and she came up with some creative ways for him to earn money to pay back all the stamps he used.

I can't say how many young people Bertie's Buddies has really helped. And to me, it doesn't really matter, because regardless of how many kids have learned how to be better friends, its greatest achievement can be seen on the faces of Mr. and Mrs. Godspeed. When Nerissa and I walked into the community center where the Bertie's Buddies main office is (the center was built on the former location of the store where Bertie was shot), the Godspeeds were talking to a small group of people who I later learned were local business leaders who were being courted to donate money for the organization's educational outreach efforts.

I didn't want to interrupt the Godspeeds in the middle of a meeting, but one thing I learned in my short career of working at a law firm is that time is a precious commodity, and even though I don't believe that the ultimate gauge of how well you're spending your time is how much money you've extracted from clients in the form of billable hours, I do know that moments you spend just hanging around and waiting are opportunities you'll never get back.

Before I could make any decisions on what to do next, Nerissa and I turned around at the sound of our names being called. Esme Solombe, Mrs. Godspeed's longtime assistant, greeted us, hugged us, and showed us over to a little nook in the wall with a coffeemaker and refrigerator. After Nerissa accepted coffee and I selected a lemon seltzer water and a banana, which were just barely enough to blunt my increasingly distracting hunger pains, Esme explained that they'd been juggling conflicting schedules for weeks to line up a time when all of these potential donors could show up to hear the Godspeeds' pitch for a new plan to help kids in need, and today was the only time all month when they were all free for an hour and willing to sit and learn why it was worthwhile for them to hand over their beloved cash.

"It's actually lucky that these potential donors came to visit when they did," Esme declared as she poured hot water from a dispenser and added a teabag. "With everything that's been going on, I think that this is a great distraction."

"Have you heard from the police investigating the identity theft lately?" Nerissa asked.

"No. I called them yesterday at Mr. Godspeed's request, and Mrs. Godspeed called them too, but they haven't gotten back to us. I hate to say it, but I know this is taking a major emotional toll." Esme's voice dipped, and she leaned forwards towards us after a quick look to make sure no one was listening. "The wastebasket's full of tissues. I know she's been crying in private. I didn't want to say anything to her face. I wanted to ask her more, but I had to double back to my actual job to help my new boss with an emergency."

"New boss, Esme? Did you change jobs?"

She nodded. "I just switched jobs a couple of weeks ago, actually. I was working as a personal assistant for the owner of an auto parts company for a while, but it wasn't a good employment environment. My boss was a little too… attentive, and it was making me uncomfortable, so it took a while, but I found a better job assisting the owner of a few local restaurants. Better pay, closer to my apartment, and aside from the occasional sudden emergency I need to defuse during the dinner hours, way better all around. Tina, my new boss, is great, and not nearly as handsy as my last employer. Still, if the Godspeeds could afford to pay me, I'd be working here full time, but…." She shrugged. "There's not much money to be made in helping out kids in trouble. Have you heard about our new initiatives?"

I had, but Nerissa hadn't. "Mrs. Godspeed started to tell me out them last night, but before she could go into details, the conversation turned to… other topics."

Esme understood. "Well, we're branching out to help kids in challenging situations in other ways. We did some brainstorming recently on major problems affecting young people, and we decided to address child hunger. For a lot of kids, the only really good meal they get is the school lunch, and there are already some organizations trying to keep kids suffering from food insecurity to provide lunches during the summer, but we started wondering, what about the weekends? A lot of kids aren't getting substantial, healthy meals on Saturday and Sunday. So we're trying to figure out ways to get them fed, and we're starting a kind of Meals on Wheels program for kids—and their families too, for that matter—to be distributed on Saturday and Sunday afternoons. That's why we've got all of those potential donors here right now. We need funding for the food and containers and maybe some of those big insulated carriers to keep them warm during the deliveries. We're going to start small, with a list of fifty or sixty kids in need in a limited area. If it works as we hope it will, we'll increase by another couple of dozen every month. My new boss is here, you know. We're hoping she can donate some takeout containers and maybe some leftovers from Friday and Saturday night shifts, too."

Esme was a bit breathless. She looked as if the excitement over this new endeavor was bubbling up inside her, and she couldn't control her happiness over all the good they'd be doing in the near future.

"That sounds like a really worthy plan," Nerissa remarked.

"Yeah, and…" Esme's voice trailed off, and the joy in her face faded dramatically as a familiar figure exited from the room where the Godspeeds were meeting with donors. He was a tall, lean, and smarmy man, well-known to all Milwaukeeans who followed the local news. His name was Tyler Coquina, and he had ambitions to be a major mover and shaker in the city. By all accounts, he was not a rich man, but he dressed as if he didn't need to keep an eye on his credit card bill. He wasn't quite forty yet, and he had the easy self-confidence of a man who believes he's much more charming than he really is. He'd started a few small businesses—mostly food trucks—over the years, all of which had been quickly sold at a loss, though no one seemed to know just how deeply in the red he'd gotten. Not a single election in the last decade had passed without him running for mayor or comptroller or alderman or city council or something else, and without fail, the voters had politely but firmly informed him that his services would not be needed. Lately, he'd tried to build up a reputation for himself as a kind of philanthropist, but due to his financial situation, his philanthropy was devoted to encouraging other, more affluent people to open up their checkbooks. He was actually a pretty skilled fundraiser, and could probably have gotten a decent job as a development officer for some avaricious college, but he was determined to pursue his own career course, and given my own erratic pathway to making a living, I'm in no position to criticize anybody else for following an unconventional road to success.

What did churn my stomach was the way he made no attempt to hide his leer at Nerissa as he walked towards us. I was trying to come up with a suitably scathing remark to direct at him, but Nerissa shot me the look that she has many times before, the one that says "Relax. I've got this."

As Tyler approached us, Nerissa gave him a tight-lipped smile that was in no way reflected in her eyes, and said, "Hello, Tyler. How's your wife doing?"

The shameless can't be chastised. "She's fine. But not as fine as you're looking today, Nerissa."

If it were possible to bottle the oiliness of that man, America's dependence on foreign petroleum would be forever ended. I'm pretty sure he genuinely believed he was irresistibly charming.

I didn't mind his ignoring my presence one bit. The longer I could go without having to converse with him, the better. Besides, watching Nerissa handle a lecher is more entertaining than ninety percent of what's on television.

Tyler stretched out a hand in Nerissa's direction, but before he could get his grubby mitt within two feet of her, she halted him with a polite yet blunt "Did you wash your hands after the last time you used the bathroom?"

That froze him. "I... think so."

"Best to be sure, isn't it? You wouldn't want to treat a woman like a dirty rag used to clean out a toilet, would you? Better find a sink."

Looking nonplussed, Tyler wandered away. I didn't believe that he was going to attend to his personal hygiene, but he was out of our hair for the time being.

"You handled him perfectly," Esme informed Nerissa.

"Thanks," Nerissa fingered the lapels of her caramel-colored leather jacket. "This is one of my favorites, and I'd hate to have to burn it after he touched it."

"I agree. Well done." An elegant-looking woman who spent more on the care and maintenance of her hair than most people do on their homes in a decade sashayed into the break room. This was Vianne Coquina. She'd been married to Tyler for a little over four years, no children yet. Neither I nor anybody else in my acquaintance knew anything about her background, or why she chose to link her life with Tyler's, especially since she never seemed to display any warmth or affection towards her husband, at least in public. I was curious as to what brought and kept them together, but I make it a rule to only poke my nose into other people's marriages when I'm hired to do so, and I consider that a very wise policy indeed.

Vianne stroked her hair and leaned against the wall. "The Godspeeds gave a great presentation, Esme. Everybody's really impressed and enthusiastic to contribute to the project."

Esme grinned. "Thanks. I worked all week on it."

"All by yourself?"

The question made Esme look uneasy, as if she'd been caught inadvertently denigrating the Godspeeds. "Well, we started planning the presentation earlier this week, but I took over the last few days because…you know… they've been distracted with what's been happening lately with their late son's identity being stolen."

Vianne's face fell a bit. "Yes, I heard about that. Terrible. Anyway, my husband has gotten in touch with his contacts, and he thinks he can donate at least ten thousand dollars of other people's money to the kids' Meals on Wheels program."

"How does that work?" Nerissa's eyebrows are naturally pretty severe, and I don't know how she managed to make them arch, but she did.

The joyless chuckle from Vianne just made me even more curious about what kept their marriage going. "Have you ever heard how the most successful Broadway producers work? Their cardinal rule is to never put their own money into one of the shows they back. They find other rich people to put up the funds and give them a cut of the proceeds from the show, keeping a nice slice of the profits for themselves. That's how Tyler works. He hits up wealthy individuals to give their cash to charity."

"And like Broadway producers, does he make money from the deal?" I couldn't help but ask.

"No, but I don't resent your wondering about that. Tyler can't keep his hands off pretty women, but he never dips his fingers into the kitty. Tyler profits from good publicity. When there's a photo op of donors presenting a check to a hospital, he makes sure he's in it. When charities hand out cheap plaques to donors, he makes sure he gets his. We've got a whole wall at home that's totally covered with the damn things." Vianne looked at me with an amused expression. "Are you going to question me, Mr. Suspicious-Minded Private Investigator?"

"Is there something I should be suspecting you for, Vianne?" As a matter of fact, she was on my list of suspects. I knew she was on the board of directors for Bertie's Buddies, and it was possible that she had been there at the meeting that Mrs. Godspeed had mentioned the previous night, where a folder containing Bertie's personal information had been left out on the table.

"I know that the Godspeeds believe that whoever stole Bertie's private information got it at a recent meeting. I know you'll be digging into that meeting, so I'll spare you the trouble. Yes, I was there that day. Yes, I saw the folder with Bertie's information on the table. No, I didn't look inside. No, I'm not involved in any identity theft. No, I don't have any idea who would have taken that information. No, I don't suspect anybody else at the meeting. All of the other members of the board are lovely people, and dear Esme would never be involved in anything so sordid as ghosting a teenaged murder victim. Personally, I'm convinced that the identity thief got the details on Bertie's life some other way, because no one at that meeting would have done it."

"That's true," Esme chimed in. "The other three board members at the meeting were Mrs. Blithe, Mrs. Dalby, and Mrs. Tabbets, and they're all sweet old ladies with fourteen grandchildren between them. I don't think any of them have ever heard of identity theft."

"Everybody's heard of identity theft," I countered. "Lots of older people are familiar with it because advertisers for personal information security warn about the need to prevent identity theft during the commercials for the shows that senior citizens watch. Every syndicated episode of *Murder, She Wrote* is punctuated by ads telling viewers to watch out for people trying to swipe their Social Security Numbers. I talked with some elderly alumni about security issues lately, and they were all more concerned about identity theft than they were about prostate cancer."

"Hmm." I couldn't tell what Vianne was thinking. "I suppose you're right. All those old people worked their whole lives to build up a nest egg, and now that they're both hoping not to die and worried that they might outlive their savings, they're petrified that someone will take away their hopes for a comfortable retirement." She shuddered. "I rather hope that I don't get old."

"The alternative's not that great either," I quipped.

"Maybe," Vianne adjusted her pink blazer and looked over towards the meeting room. "Don't ever tell the Godspeeds I said this, but sometimes I think that poor Bertie was lucky. When you're a kid, you think that life's going to be an endless parade of opportunities and excitement, and achievement. Then you go through years of agonizing puberty, and by the time everything settles down, you meet up with one disappointment after another. If I'd ever known what was ahead of me when I was a kid, I'd never have been in a rush to get past thirteen."

"That…is pretty bleak," Esme replied.

"But it's true." Vianne gestured towards the large gold crucifix, and the silver Miraculous Medal Nerissa always wears. "You're a believer, I see."

"Yes. We just came from Mass."

"I wish I could believe in something. But experience won't let me. With everything the way it is in the world, how can I possibly accept that some all-knowing power is in charge of the universe?"

"My uncle gets asked that a lot," I answered. "His standard response is that "God is not your butler." It's amazing how people think that an all-powerful and all-knowing entity should be required to make sure everything is nice and pleasant, and comfortable for you. There's something rather ridiculous in trying to make a deity your servant and making belief contingent on having everything your own way. And after all, what we think is the perfect situation for us may not really be as great as we think it will be for ourselves and others."

Vianne stood silent for a few moments and then replied, "Well, I'm not here to talk theology. I should check in on my husband and see if he's cornered any other unfortunate women." She pivoted on the heel of her designer shoe and walked away with the briefest of goodbyes.

"I'm not the only one wondering what specific disappointments she was referring to, am I?" Esme whispered. Nerissa and I assured her that she was not. "Good."

"Esme, can you email me a list of the people who were at the meeting we were talking about earlier, along with their contact information, please?" I asked.

"Yes. But, again, I don't think any of them would have anything to do with identity theft. And I thought you weren't supposed to interfere with an open police investigation?"

"Who's interfering? All I'm doing is a little security work for my friends. Of course, if I were to find something, I'd pass it on to the police immediately."

Nerissa bit her lip, checked to make sure she couldn't be overheard, and whispered to the two of us, "Shifting the subject a bit, how did the Coquinas get involved in Bertie's Buddies?"

"I have no idea," Esme whispered back. "One day about a year ago, they showed up, started gushing about what wonderful work we were doing helping kids in need, and before we knew it, Tyler was hosting fundraisers, and Vianne was on the board of directors. I don't even think she was offered a position. She just stated that she wished to be on the board, and there you go."

"I bet you're not the first charity to have that happen to them," I remarked. "I know that she's on the boards of at least a dozen other nonprofits, and I wouldn't be surprised if she got her place on them the same way."

Nerissa sniffed. "Such charitable people."

"You two volunteer a lot for all sorts of things. Why are you so suspicious of someone else giving back to the community?"

Esme's question was a fair one, but Nerissa was clearly displeased by it. "Look me in the eye and tell me that the Coquinas genuinely care about Milwaukee's kids."

"Point taken. But they've given us so much money, and I don't think we should question their motives when all they've done is help us."

I heard the sound of several people walking out and saying their goodbyes, and as I stepped out to take a look, I saw the potential donors leaving the building, the Coquinas among them. Esme hurried out to speak with her new boss. Not knowing any of them or feeling the need to exchange pleasantries, Nerissa and I waited a few moments and then joined the Godspeeds.

Both of them had radiant smiles. "They loved our plan. Altogether, they pledged more than three times what we were hoping for," Mrs. Godspeed gushed.

"That's great!"

"Indeed it is, Isaiah. We may be able to do weekend meals on wheels for over three hundred kids now. But we're going to need your help."

"What can I do, Mr. Godspeed?"

"Well, I hate to impose, but before our donors make their official donations, we're going to have to demonstrate that our plan is viable. They want to see us make a test run. Esme's boss is going to make a bunch of lasagnas and salads, and we've got a list of young people who suffer from food insecurity, so next Saturday...."

"You want me to help with deliveries?"

"Could you please? A couple of other people will be covering different areas. If you started around noon, you could be done in time for Saturday Mass. You'd have about forty kids on your route, and they all live within the same square mile. It should take three hours at most. We'll phone ahead and confirm that everybody's there. You'll be riding with a few of our donors, so they can see what you're doing firsthand."

I silently hoped that I wouldn't have Tyler Coquina as my ride-along.

The Godspeeds filled us in on the details of their just-concluded meeting, and afterwards, Nerissa and I helped them wrap a bunch of toys and clothes that were donated for their birthday present program. Once we'd gotten a month's worth of free gifts covered in shiny paper, properly labeled and marked with sticky notes to clarify when they needed to be delivered, and stacked them in order by date in a storage room, Nerissa and I congratulated the Godspeeds on their successful presentation again, confirmed we'd see them in a week, and marched into the parking lot just in time to see a disheveled man trying to break into Nerissa's sports car with a slim jim.

Nerissa started to turn purple with rage at the violation. Normally I like that color on her, but not in this context. I gave the guy a quick look-over, determined that he probably wasn't carrying a weapon, and quickly walked up behind him. The would-be carjacker's physique was frail in the way that people become when they consume more meth than protein, and after seeing his face reflected in the driver-side window, I really hoped that he wouldn't put up a fight because first, I believe that violence should be used sparingly and only in self-defense when all other options have been exhausted; and second, this man had so few teeth remaining that I doubted I could morally justify a punch that might cost him both of his precious remaining molars. I did put my hand around his wrist, as I didn't want him to poke me in the eye with the slim jim. "Sir, I'd appreciate it if you'd please stop trying to break into my girlfriend's car immediately. If you put even an eighth-of-an-inch-long scratch on it, she'll respond in a way that will not be pleasant for you or the emergency room employees who'll have to patch you up, so what say you give me that slim jim now, okay?"

The man was even more lacking in courage than he was in teeth. He slipped the slim jim into my hand and then collapsed to his knees and started crying. "Please, just let me go. Just gimme a break, will ya?"

I took an involuntary step back because I didn't want this guy soiling my coat with either his grubby hands or his salty tears. Turning to Nerissa, I asked her, "What do you think? Shall we send him on his way?"

The sun was sinking fast, so Nerissa pulled out the little flashlight she keeps on her key ring and examined her car. "No damage. Thank God we came out when we did." Her face was back to its normal color, but I could see the thirst for vengeance in her eyes. "Maybe he should spend the night in a cell. It'll teach him a lesson."

I was hoping she wouldn't feel this way, and not because I was suddenly oozing the milk of human kindness from my pores. The quality of mercy may not have been strained, but my stomach was kicking up a royal tantrum over the way I'd been ignoring it today. Turning this guy in to the police would mean filling out a report, and at least an hour, probably two or more, down the drain. I needed a hot square meal way more than I wanted to see him behind bars. I was trying to convey this point to Nerissa through my eyes, as I wanted to keep up a show of strength and intimidation towards this fellow for as long as possible.

"Please, just let me walk away. I'll never touch another car again." I knew he was lying, just babbling in order to placate me, but before I could confront him with his mendacity, he flung out his arms, and an envelope fell out of the pocket of his jeans, which were so full of holes they barely qualified as pants. "I swear that if you let me go–" He flung out his arms in what was presumably a gesture of supplication, and an envelope shot out of one of the sleeves of his tattered jacket and got caught in a gust of wind that sent it flying upwards. I was surprised that Nerissa was able to make the leap she did while wearing her favorite ankle boots with three-inch heels, but she jumped, grabbed the envelope, and returned to the ground without so much as a wobble. I was impressed.

Nerissa glanced at the envelope, and the facial expression she made was something I'd never seen before or since. She turned to the kneeling miscreant with a look of both accusation and horror and demanded to know, "Where did you get this?"

The man at my feet hesitated for a moment, and then leapt up, whirled around, and raced away. He disappeared around a corner, and though he only had a couple of seconds of a head start on me, by the time I could see around the corner, he was nowhere to be found. My hunting instinct prodded me to keep looking for him, but my empty stomach shrewdly reminded me that without the need to take that fellow to the police station, I could sit down to a nice meal a lot sooner.

I returned to Nerissa and updated her on what had happened. I was a bit surprised she hadn't chased after the guy as well, but the weird look on her face told me that something about the envelope had blindsided her. "What's going on with that envelope?"

"Look at it." She handed it to me. There were no creases, though it had a very slight bow in it, and an uncancelled stamp featuring an orange kitten was affixed neatly in the right corner. It was sealed with no return address.

But what had presumably caught Nerissa's attention was the mailing address. It was supposed to be sent to a P.O. box in Green Bay. The name of the addressee was Bertie Godspeed.

I couldn't see my own face, but I assumed it looked just Nerissa's, only a lot less pretty.

"What the heck?"

Nerissa's question was a considerably bowdlerized version of what was flashing through my mind at that moment.

"It couldn't be another Bertie Godspeed," I muttered. "I did an Internet search for his name the other day, and all the links were connected to Bertie's Buddies. I ran some variants like "Bert" and "Bertram" and even "Cuthbert." There's no one else with that name. But where did he get it? Was he sending it? Could he have found it on the ground?"

"Unlikely. Look at how clean the envelope is." Nerissa pointed. "The spring thaw means pretty much every surface on the ground outside is covered in mud, slush, dirty water, and salt residue."

I nodded. At that moment, I was less interested in where the guy had gotten it than I was in what was inside, and said so.

"Can you even open it, Funderburke? Isn't that interfering with the mail?"

"It bears no evidence of having entered the hands of the U.S. Postal Service. But we can see the addressee, and we can ask his presumed next of kin." I marched back inside the building, with Nerissa right behind me. The Godspeeds and Esme were putting on their coats.

"Is something wrong, Isaiah?"

Until that moment, I hadn't bothered to think about how this envelope might have affected the Godspeeds. Seeing their late son's name printed on a letter bound for Green Bay might provoke unpleasant reactions. "Mr. and Mrs. Godspeed, I'm going to ask you to trust my judgment right now. May I please have your permission to open this envelope?"

"Yes, of course. But what's in it? Where did you get it?"

"I'll explain in a minute." I hurried over to the break room, and plugged the hot water kettle back into the wall. Momentarily, it started steaming again, and I held the envelope in the steam, and soon afterwards, I was able to peel back the now-unsealed flap with a little gentle easing with the slim jim I suddenly realized I was still holding.

Inside was a note written in block letters, saying:

K–

I'LL SEND MORE IN A FEW DAYS. STAY WHERE YOU ARE AND DON'T GO OUT EXCEPT TO THE CORNER STORE TO GET FOOD AND ACROSS THE STREET TO CHECK THE POST OFFICE BOX. DON'T USE THE BURNER PHONE UNTIL I SAY YOU CAN. REMEMBER, DON'T CHECK YOUR EMAIL, DON'T GO ON THE INTERNET, AND DON'T USE MY STREAMING SUBSCRIPTION. YOU CAN WATCH REGULAR TV AND GO WITHOUT CABLE FOR A LITTLE LONGER. TRUST ME. I KNOW YOU'RE SCARED, BUT THIS IS THE ONLY CHOICE YOU HAVE. FOR ONCE IN YOUR LIFE, PLEASE LISTEN TO ME.

LOVE,

G

The note was written on an ordinary sheet of white computer paper. There was nothing distinctive about it or the black ink. What was notable was the contents: sixty dollars in three twenty-dollar bills.

I was so caught up in my own thoughts, I didn't realize that four other people were watching me. "What is that?" Mr. Godspeed asked.

Part of me still didn't want to upset the Godspeeds, but the part of my brain that could prevaricate was frozen, and I found myself explaining exactly what had happened. It only took a minute. The news didn't have quite the effect that I thought it would on the Godspeeds. They seemed to accept this new twist without any visible distress. I realized that there'd probably be a delayed reaction effect here.

Mrs. Godspeed was the first to respond. "Can you describe the man who tried to break into Nerissa's car?"

I nodded. "Clearly a drug user. He looked like he could be fifty, but given the life he's been living, he could well be in his thirties. Less fat on him than a lettuce leaf, doesn't need dental floss because his few remaining teeth are so far apart, not that he eats much anyway. Couldn't determine his eye color because his pupils were so dilated. Badly cut sandy hair, thinning on top. Dark bags under eyes, a couple of open sores on his left cheek. Wearing jeans with so many holes you could see more skin on his legs than denim, wearing a tan hoodie that was eight or nine sizes too big for him. All the perfumes of Arabia wouldn't sweeten the rotting stench coming from the poor blighter."

"That's Dallan. I don't know his last name. He hangs around this neighborhood. He roots through trash cans, begs for money or food, and sometimes he tries to steal things." Mrs. Godspeed sighed. "He stole my purse once, and as he tried to sprint away, he ran into a lamppost and knocked himself out. I give him some soft food and milk a few times a week."

"How do you think he got that?" Esme asked.

"I'd have to look into it. And since there's an open investigation going on, I think I'd need to send this to the police in Chicago. Is that all right with you?"

The Godspeeds agreed and gave me the phone numbers of the officers who'd visited them a few days ago. I called the first one and left a message. The second was somewhat under-enthused, made it clear that he was juggling more cases than he could handle, and asked me to mail the letter to him. He provided me with an address, and I promised to send the letter to him, though I made sure to photograph the envelope and its contents for my own personal use first.

While my instincts balked at his lack of enthusiasm, instead of complaining, I stuffed the letter and money into a manila envelope provided to me by the Godspeeds, stamped and addressed it, and after Esme promised to drop it off in a mailbox for me, I wished the Godspeeds and Esme good night.

"Yes, we'd better get home. Zita's at my sister Yolanda's house, and she wanted to make sure we picked Zita up by six so she could go to a movie with her friends. Thanks again for your help tonight, Isaiah."

As soon as her husband finished talking, Mrs. Godspeed put her hand on my shoulder. "Don't go investigating that Post Office box on your own, Isaiah.

Leave it to the police. I know you want to find out what happened yourself, but please. Focus on living your life instead of avenging your friend."

I gave her a noncommittal hug goodbye, and as soon as Nerissa and I were back in her car, Nerissa turned to me and asked, "You haven't had a proper meal all day. Do you want to go to that new Thai restaurant for dinner?"

I nodded. As Nerissa pulled out of the parking lot, she sighed and said, "I know you're not going to be able to resist following up this lead yourself."

Turning my new slim jim over in my hands, I answered, "You know me so well, Nerissa."

"Then you should know I'll be helping you."

"Thank you. That's much appreciated."

"Promise me you'll take a little break from this, though? Can we not talk about this case until after we eat?"

"That's a good idea." We drove along the rapidly darkening street, and I forced myself not to ponder who was living in Green Bay, using Bertie's name.

Chapter Five

A Reason to Get Up in the Morning

Nerissa was right. I needed a break to clear my head. Ever since Zita had walked into my office and told me about Bertie being ghosted, I'd been remembering memories I was better off keeping out of my mind. From the ages of eight to thirteen, from the middle of third grade to the middle of seventh grade, which is from the time my mother and the man I thought was my father started their divorce (which was so lengthy and malicious it made the Hundred Years War look like a brief tiff), to the time that I finally moved out of my mother's and her noxious second husband's home and into my grandparents' house. This was not an easy four years for me. I could go into details, but every second I spend typing up an account about that terrible period is a second I relive that era, and why should I inject poison into my own veins if I can avoid it?

So I distracted myself, and Nerissa and I went to dinner. I made up for the meals I missed earlier in the day, and as usual, Nerissa stopped eating long before she was full and spent the rest of the evening watching me consume my food with an envious expression. We chatted about television shows and books we'd been reading and resolutely ignored anything that might be considered serious. I talked about my theories on how to increase one's chances of winning on some of my favorite old game shows, like *Classic Concentration* and *Supermarket Sweep*, and Nerissa contributed some insightful feedback as to my reasoning, and provided some tips of her own, such as waiting a bit for other contestants to grab the three Shopping List items in order to make it easier to spot them by the gaps in the store shelves. Nerissa discussed some recent items of clothing she'd purchased, and the outfits she planned to wear in the near future, such as the brand new metallic copper pantsuit she'd found on eBay for fifteen bucks, the cranberry oversized turtleneck she planned to pair with a chocolate-brown ankle-length suede skirt, and the new green satin blouse with an embossed snakeskin pattern she'd discovered in a bargain bin for two dollars and would soon be worn with one of her countless pairs of black lambskin trousers, but she was still deciding which one. Personally, my interest in fashion is so infinitesimally minuscule that the world's most powerful electron microscope couldn't detect its presence, though I do love seeing Nerissa wearing her outfits. The closest I come to planning my clothes choices in advance is making sure I still have plenty of clean pants. I choose my shirts in the morning by reaching into my closet with my eyes still bleary with sleep and wearing the first shirt my hand randomly touches. It's a sound system, and it has served me well over the years, allowing me to devote my precious time to pondering more valuable subjects, such as how to make the best use of a Wild Card on *Classic Concentration*.

If it weren't for the elephant in the room, this would have been a pretty good date night. As it was, it was a nice evening, but I had to work so hard at keeping everything pleasant and away from certain topics that I didn't have much fun.

After Nerissa dropped me off at home and I said good night to Mrs. Zwidecker, I plonked myself in front of my computer and started doing a little Internet sleuthing, which is increasingly one of my favorite forms of private detecting. It beats the heck out of sitting in a cold car on a stakeout with nothing but a camera, a thermos, and an empty plastic bottle to keep you company. I tracked down the post office where the letter was addressed. The note mentioned that the addressee was staying across the street, and there was a corner store. A little time studying an online map, and I found a neighborhood that fit the description. Aside from a couple of fast-food restaurants and giant parking lots, there was only an inexpensive chain motel in a one-block radius. That looked like a likely place for an identity thief to hide.

A rush of triumph swept over me, and I debated my next course of action. Every atom of my body wanted to jump in my car, drive up to Green Bay, and track down the identity thief. I jingled my keys in my hand for a while, gently reminding myself that I didn't know which room the suspect was staying in, and I couldn't very well knock on every door, rousing the adulterers and drug users and sequestered jurors, asking them if they'd ghosted a kid named Bertie Godspeed who'd been murdered well over a decade ago.

After fifteen minutes of jingling, I tossed my keys back in the little wooden bowl that had been carved by one of my students, who'd made it with his father as a gift to thank me for clearing his innocent dad of an insider trading accusation (it was the secretary who made the shady deals all on her own). I realized I hadn't taken off my coat, and I decided that it was just as well, as I went outside to take a brisk walk around the block to burn off some nervous energy. Twelve laps later, I was back in the house. I picked up a book, and twenty pages later, I realized I couldn't remember a word I'd read. I turned on the TV, and after a lot of channel surfing, I failed to find anything worth watching, and none of the vast hours of programming I'd saved on the digital recorder interested me either. I played a few games on my tablet, realized I was still wearing my coat, and decided that even though it was barely after nine, and I'd only been up for a shade over five hours, I should consider going to bed.

Of course, the journey from deciding to call it a night and actually falling asleep can be a lengthy one. I showered, felt like I should get some sort of work done, and quickly realized I was good for nothing. I had a ton of pent-up energy, and no focus to do anything with it. In any case, sitting in front of a device with wi-fi access would simply drive me into a state of Internet trance, where time passes mindlessly without anything productive actually getting done.

I was in a highly worked-up state of mind, which is when Uncle Francis tells me I should be praying instead of fuming. I took his advice for a few minutes, and when I finally got up from kneeling on my bed, my head was clearer and inspiration had struck. I crossed to my desk, pulled out a sheet of paper and a pen, and wrote the following letter in black ink in block letters.

K–
I'M DEALING WITH A TRICKY SITUATION. I CAN'T SEND MONEY NOW FOR REASONS I'LL EXPLAIN LATER. I NEED TO SEE YOU FACE-TO-FACE. I'LL GIVE YOU SOME MONEY THEN. THIS IS BIG. YOU'LL UNDERSTAND EVERYTHING WHEN I TELL YOU. TEXT ME AT THIS NUMBER ON YOUR BURNER PHONE AS SOON AS YOU GET THIS. DON'T CALL. TEXT. SEE YOU SOON.
LOVE,
G

I keep a few burner phones in my desk. I jotted down the number for one of them at the end of the letter, reread my work, folded it up, and stuck it in an envelope, which I sealed, stamped, and addressed. With a satisfied nod, I crossed back to my bed, flopped back on it, and asked myself, "What do I do now?"

Either God or my body or both told me that what I really needed to do was get even more sleep. After an indeterminate but surprisingly short period of time staring at my ceiling, the next thing I knew it was ten-thirty in the morning, and I had fifteen minutes to get ready for Sunday Mass with Nerissa and the Kaiming family. I drove myself that day, stopping by a mailbox to send the note I'd written the previous night.

The "no talking about the whole Bertie situation" rule continued through the Sunday afternoon meal with the Kaimings, until I was saying my goodbyes, and Keith took me aside.

"Nerissa told me what happened last night," he informed me.

"I'm guessing you're not referring to how many Thai spring rolls I ate," I quipped.

"No, I'm talking about the letter and money you found."

"What about it?"

"Last night, when I was trying to get the youngest kids settled back in bed after they woke up simultaneously and demanded water, I thought about that letter, and I wondered what you were doing about it. I considered the possibility that you'd just leave it to the police, and rejected it."

"You know me well."

"I do. And then I pondered further, and realized that your plan of action would be to write your own letter and send it along to that address, telling the recipient to meet you somewhere or something like that."

I sass a lot of people, but I would never disrespect Keith, especially with a lie. "Or, just tell him to send a text to one of my burner phones."

"Uh-huh. So the question now is, have you actually sent that letter?"

"Yes. Yes, I have. Are you going to warn me to be careful?"

"You know all that, Funderburke. I just have one question for you. Don't you think this all seems just a little bit convenient?"

"How do you mean, convenient?"

"Point one. You run into this Dallan guy in the parking lot, right after a crowd of donors for Bertie's Buddies leaves. Isn't it an odd coincidence that Dallan didn't enter the parking lot until only the cars belonging to Nerissa, the Godspeeds, and Esme were there? Just think, if he'd come five minutes earlier, he'd have had his pick of the donors' cars, and given how much money we know they have, you'd think their automobiles would reflect their bank accounts, wouldn't you?"

"Yeah... Bad timing on Dallan's part that he missed those cars...." I started rifling through my mental files on crime statistics. "I checked Nerissa's car. He didn't even scratch the paint, which is hard when you have shaking, meth-addled hands. It takes a bit of dexterity to use a slim jim, especially in fading light. A lot of addicts don't use slim jims unless they're planning to take the entire car. If they just want to swipe the contents of the automobile, they smash and grab. They're more likely to carry a hammer or wrench than a slim jim."

"Good point. And then there's the fact that this letter addressed to "Bertie Godspeed" came flying out of his sleeve. What was he doing with it? Is he involved in the ghosting? You said he had shaky hands. If the penmanship on the letter was nice and neat, he couldn't have written it. Did he find it or steal it? Why would anybody ask him to mail it? What are the odds that the person breaking into Nerissa's car just as you're walking out to catch him would be carrying an envelope he'd planned to mail, or alternatively, found or stole from the identity thief that bore a name that would mean something to only a tiny handful of people in Milwaukee? And how minuscule are the chances that two of those people would come across it? And how likely is the possibility that the envelope would come flying out of his sleeve at just that moment? Why was it in his sleeve, where it could easily slip out, instead of folded up in his pocket? The whole thing reeks of stagecraft."

My brain's gears whirred and clicked for a while, and the answer they produced was, "Someone paid Dallan to pretend to break into Nerissa's car as we were leaving, get caught by me, and drop that envelope where I'd find it. But who and why? Is someone trying to lure me into some kind of trap?"

"If someone wanted to harm you, why pay a meth addict to drop an envelope in front of you? Why not hire someone to come after you in that parking lot with a bat or a gun? Maybe this isn't a trap so much as a trail of breadcrumbs."

"Could someone involved with the ghosting operation be having pangs of conscience? Someone's trying to leak information that could lead to my finding out the identity of the identity thieves?"

"Perhaps. But what would be the point of writing that letter from an anxious-sounding person to a supposed loved one who seems to be in danger? Why not just send you an actual letter or an email telling you exactly what was going on and who was involved? Just cut out the runaround and give you all the information you need. It's way easier."

"That's a great point."

"But why would someone write to you anyway? Wouldn't it make more sense to tell the police? Who even knows you'd have an interest in finding out who's ghosting Bertie? That's not public knowledge."

I've often told Keith that if he ever gets tired of teaching, he might want to consider going into private detection. He has a great mind for it.

I thought about his questions for a while and came up with no answers.

Before I left, Nerissa and I spent twenty minutes helping Toby through her math homework, and then the three of us played a quick game of Scrabble. They both hugged me goodbye as I left and, halfway to my car, Toby called out, "Funderburke?"

"Yeah?"

"Take care of yourself. You look distracted. I don't want anything to happen to you."

"I will, kid. Thanks."

"Can we talk for a moment?"

"Sure. Did you want to talk in my car?"

"Please. It'll only take a few minutes."

Nerissa, who was back inside, shot me a quizzical look through the window. I shrugged to let her know I didn't know what Toby wanted to talk to me about, and turning to Toby asked, "So, what's up?"

"I have a problem that I don't want the rest of the family to know. It's not serious. But I feel embarrassed, though I think you'll understand."

"Okay. What is it?"

"A boy asked me out."

I'd been tensing up, but I immediately relaxed. "That's certainly not a bad thing, but I know how uncomfortable it can be to talk about with your family. You know that you can tell Nerissa or Keith or Midge or any of your other relatives anything."

"I know. I don't understand why this is so difficult."

"Well, nothing to do with boy/girl relationships at this age is easy. Or at any other age, for that matter."

"Sounds like the future's pretty bright."

"That's life. The sooner you realize how messy things can get, the better. So what's the issue. Don't you like him?"

"Yeah, sort of. I don't have a full-fledged crush on him or anything, but he's nice and cute and even though I only really like him as a friend, I think that he'd be a good guy to see a movie with, maybe get ice cream later... That's what he suggested."

"That's a fun plan."

"But it's Mom–" Toby took a deep breath and continued. "You know I'm just about the same age she was when she... and also when her mother...."

"I know."

"That's not going to happen to me. I'm not going to let anything happen with us. I don't think he'd even try anyway."

I wasn't quite so certain, but I said nothing.

"But I want a chaperone and don't want Mom—to spend the whole time giving him the stink eye. Do you think he'll mind if I ask that his parents, or at least one of them, join us?"

"They'll be driving you, won't they? Though they can probably sit a couple of rows behind you at the theater."

"That's an idea. Can you talk to Mom about this tomorrow? Let her know that it's okay to let me go out and that she's not going to become a grandmother anytime soon."

"Of course."

"Maybe calm her down? You know how she can get."

"She knew this day would come. We've talked about it."

"Good. But not tonight. I'm not mentally ready for The Talk."

"Fine, Toby. If she calls and asks me, what do I say?"

"You'll tell her tomorrow."

"And if she asks you tonight?"

"I'll tell her I was asking your advice on how to tell one of my friends with divorced parents how to prevent being shipped off to boarding school."

"No, don't lie—" My efforts to admonish her failed, as Toby had already skipped out of the car and hurried back inside the house. I hesitated and then drove away.

When I got back home, I changed and made my way to the local pool. Sometimes a sustained burst of physical energy is just what I need to get my analytical processes going properly.

The pool was fairly empty, aside from a lifeguard and three tough-looking elderly Eastern European women who simply leaned against one edge of the pool and floated, talking rapidly in a language I didn't understand. They're there every time I come to swim, and I've never seen them leave that little corner of the pool except to leave for the day. Though they've never done this in real life in my presence, in my imagination, I always picture them smoking cigarettes as they float, and I imagine that if a lifeguard confronted them, they'd just glare upwards and say, "Vot? It's not like ve're going to set the pool on fire!"

After adjusting the bathing cap that Nerissa insists I wear to protect my hair from pool chemicals, I dived into the lane furthest from the chatting trio (this was out of courtesy, as I didn't want my splashing to interrupt their conversation), and started swimming laps. Every so often, I switched styles, moving from breaststroke to backstroke to freestyle, and then shifting from sidestroke to butterfly to trudgen, and going through the list again in a different order.

At first, I tried to answer the questions Keith had posed, but I came up with a carton full of goose eggs. So I switched to thinking about some of my better memories involving Bertie, like the baking soda volcano we'd made in the fourth grade that sprayed gunk all over the classroom ceiling, the skits from *A Thurber Carnival* we'd performed in fifth grade, or the sixth-grade field trip to the Milwaukee Public Museum where one of our classmates had gotten lost, and we'd helped the teachers look for him. Turns out, he'd somehow wound up inside a broom closet that had gotten locked behind him. I'd like to say that tracking down our lost friend was my first successful case, but I didn't have anything to do with finding him. A tour guide heard him pounding on the door on the third floor while Bertie, a parent chaperone, and I were still searching the Streets of Old Milwaukee exhibit.

At one point, I rapped my knuckles on the pool's edge as I completed a lap. Not enough to bruise or fracture anything, just enough to shock me out of my own thoughts. I shook it off and switched from freestyle to butterfly. The brief distracting pain jarred a memory that had escaped my mind for a decade.

Back in sixth grade, when the situation at home was at its foulest, I'd been so frustrated with the injustice of the whole mess that while venting to Bertie, I lost control and punched a wall. It wasn't a very hard punch, and luckily for my hand, I'd hit a padded bulletin board and missed all the thumbtacks.

Still, there was a brief, sharp wave of pain that had radiated up my arm, and my more recent injury brought back the long-faded remembrance of what Bertie had said to me as I was shaking off the stinging.

"Maybe when we're grown up, we can start some organization that helps out kids like you who need assistance but don't have anybody they can turn to."

At the time, I'd nodded at Bertie's comment, thinking that what he suggested was a good idea, but even at an age when it was still considered gauche for adults to rain on our dreams of future careers as astronauts or professional athletes, I already thought a dull desk job in a poorly lit cubicle was a far more likely future than anything fun or fulfilling.

But Bertie's comment, as unlikely as it had seemed at the time, had proved amazingly prescient. I *did* make my living assisting kids who needed an ally, and I'd achieved that rare pair of career triumphs: I had a job I loved, and I was darned good at it. I was still some distance away from accomplishing the holy trinity of employment by getting a hefty paycheck, but I was doing well enough to realize that to focus on that point would be greedy.

More happy memories of adventures with my late friend continued to float through my mind, and for the first time in a few days, I looked back on the past and experienced the warm glow of reliving joyous recollections. Normally when I cast my mind back on the years from third grade to seventh grade, it's rather like eating the trail mix that Cuthbertson used to serve for dessert at lunch once a month when we were that age. We kids would root through the little paper cups to extract the pinch's worth of chocolate chips, and ignore the dusty peanuts and the hard, rubbery raisins. Searching for good times during that stage of my life is a lot like rooting for the tasty stuff amongst the stale legumes and inedible dried grapes.

But that afternoon, as I shifted from one style of swimming to the other, my brain synapses unearthed one pleasant thought after another from that era. The time we'd dug in the woods, looking for archaeological treasures. The four board games we'd invented one particularly productive summer week. The lost dog we'd found with his identification tags smeared with paint, and how we'd spent a sweltering August afternoon tracking down his owner, succeeding only minutes before dinnertime. Those were the moments that allowed me to reflect and realize that those years of my life weren't all awful.

I swam and recollected, completely losing track of time. I had just completed another lap and was flipping around to start another one when I felt a gentle poking in the small of my back. Turning around, I saw Rafe the lifeguard holding the pool skimmer. Pulling out my earplugs, I forced myself to suppress the mild asperity I was feeling and asked as politely as possible, "Something you want to say to me, Rafe?"

"Do you know how long you've been swimming, Funderburke?"

I didn't, actually. The clock is located in a corner of the room that can't be seen clearly from my end of the pool. I figured that I'd been swimming for forty-five minutes, an hour at most.

When I informed Rafe of my estimate, his jaw brushed against his ribcage. "Funderburke, buddy. You got here a little before two."

"That's right. So what time is it now?"

"It's eight-fifteen, dude. You've been in here over six and a quarter hours."

My initial response was to suspect he was playing some sort of practical joke on me, but I could detect no trace of jest in Rafe's face, and I hoisted myself out of the pool, allowed some residual water to drip off me, and crossed over to a position where I could see the clock properly. Once there, it became clear that Rafe was not messing with me.

"See, bro?" Rafe picked up my towel from the side shelves and tossed it to me.

"I don't understand. I know I was lost in thought, but how could I lose track of this much time?"

"Beats me, but you've had one heck of a workout, bro. I didn't see you stop for more than a few seconds between laps. Great stamina, dude. Good for you. I'm impressed."

It takes a lot to impress Rafe, as he's a champion swimmer who came within two and a half seconds of making it to the Olympics and hadn't given up hope on making it to the next Games, so I appreciated the compliment, though at that moment I was more concerned about my mental focus than my physical fitness. "Six hours and fifteen minutes!"

"Yeah. Your girlfriend's worried about you."

"Nerissa? You've heard from her?"

"She tried to call you for a few hours, and when she couldn't get through to you, she called Mrs. Z, who told her you'd gone to the pool earlier in the afternoon. So she phoned here and asked us to tell you she wanted you to come by the house as soon as possible, dude. Also, she wants you to stop by the drugstore and pick up Toby's allergy medication. We're gonna shut down for the night soon anyway, you know. Oh, and make sure to drink a lot of water. Just because you're a pool, that doesn't mean you can't get dehydrated. Look out for yourself, bro."

I thanked him for passing on the message and hurried to the locker rooms to call Nerissa and change. I had been the only one left in the pool, as the trio of floating women was gone, and the only other person besides Rafe in the area was a seventy-something man with an accent I can't place, a totally bald head, and twelve times the chest hair of the average person. He's a regular at the pool, and despite his years and significant girth, he wears a Speedo and spends most of his time hitting on the young female lifeguards. As only Rafe was on duty, the fellow was sprawled out in the hot tub, reading a newspaper with the bottom inch submerged in the water.

I called Nerissa as soon as I could get to my phone and showered as swiftly as I could, partly because I was in a hurry to see her and partly because I wanted to be done before the elderly Speedo man came in to wash off the chlorine. I was dried and dressed in record time, and after a long guzzle at the bubbler, I strolled back to my car. I swung by the drugstore, and when I reached the house, Midge showed me to the little room overlooking the garden where Nerissa does most of her dissertation writing. The shelves are filled with library books three rows deep, and there's a big table that's usually totally covered with papers and her laptop.

"How's the dissertation going?"

Nerissa shrugged. "I wrote three pages this evening and realized that two and a half pages of what I wrote was total garbage, so I deleted the rotten stuff."

"That's something."

"Not enough. I don't know why this is taking me so long." She looked me up and down. "You haven't had dinner yet, have you?"

"No. Nothing since you saw me last."

Midge smiled. "It's lasagna night. I'll fix you a plate."

"Thanks. Can I get some extra water to drink, please?"

"Sure." Midge left while Nerissa and I cleared a couple of stacks of books off a little end table in the corner, and I sank into the chair next to it.

"You look tired."

"I swam for over six hours straight without realizing it. I think I'm losing my grip, what with everything going on."

"Seriously? You were in the pool all this time?"

"I was thinking about Bertie. I don't know how the hours slipped away for me."

"Huh. Do you want to talk about it?"

I really didn't, and I figured it would be best to redirect the focus of the conversation. "You know, the last few days, it's all been about me and poor Bertie getting ghosted. What about you? What's going on with you? There must be something on your mind, based on your calling me and how distracted you've been with your writing. Something's bothering you, I can tell."

"What do you mean, you can tell?"

"The hair dangling down the right side of your body is all curly, the way it gets when you twist it round your finger repeatedly when there's something on your mind. Plus, you're wearing your old sweats with the Cuthbertson insignia, the ones you used to wear back in high school for soccer practice. You put those on when you're stressed out and need to get really comfortable." There was no criticism in my tone whatsoever. Nerissa looked better in those sweats than most women would in a designer ballgown.

She pulled at the collar of her sweatshirt. "I like my clothes to reflect my mood. I need something soft and non-constricting that I have a past with. I have a lot of happy memories from playing soccer."

"That's right. When I dwell on the past, I'm dealing with lingering issues. When you think about the past, you're upset about the present."

"Bingo. It's one of my girls. Tawny. You know her, right? Red hair, pretty tall?"

"Uh-huh. What about her?"

We were briefly interrupted by Midge, who brought in a tray featuring a mountain of lasagna, a bowl of Caesar salad, a large glass of milk, and a carafe of ice water with an empty glass. After admonishing me to drink all the water to rehydrate, Midge said, "I need to review an autopsy report from Jacksonville. Do you need anything else?" I declined, and Midge shut the door as she left.

"You eat, I'll talk." Nerissa said it as a statement, not a suggestion. I didn't mind a bit, as the echoing void that was my stomach, hollowed beyond endurance by over a quarter of a day's worth of swimming, needed filling fast. I munched, savored, and listened.

"You know that Tawny's parents are in the middle of a particularly rotten divorce, right?" The fullness of my mouth meant that I had to reply with a simple nod. "Well, the situation has dragged on for a very long time. That's one reason why Tawny turned to her boyfriend for comfort and got in the family way. Ever since Tawny's mother kicked Tawny's father out of the house, the mother's new boyfriend has moved in. And he's a jerk. Tawny assures me he's not physically abusive, but he's definitely verbally abusive, though he's careful to do it out of the earshot of Tawny's mother, though my gut tells me that she wouldn't make much of a fuss if she heard, anyway."

Nerissa took a deep breath, took a sip from the glass of seltzer on her desk, and continued. "But the main problem isn't with Tawny right now, but with her little sister Sabine. Have you met her?"

Swallowing my salad, I recalled that Sabine had been in the seventh-grade math class I'd substituted for a couple of months ago, and that she and Zita were friends.

"Yes, that's her." Nerissa sighed. "She's in the hospital now."

"Oh, no. What happened?"

"That's just it. Nobody knows for sure—or at least, isn't saying. Tawny found her on the bathroom floor couple of hours ago, covered in her own sick, and wouldn't wake up when she shook her, so Tawny called 911, and they rushed her to the emergency room. The doctors say she'll be all right, but they haven't figured out if she got a bad bug or...."

After Nerissa left that last thought trailing for a while, I finished the sentence for her. "If she took something?"

"Exactly. At Christmas, Tawny's mother bought a bunch of potted holly plants for decoration, and they've still got them in the sunroom."

"Holly berries are poisonous...." I muttered reflexively.

"You're a step ahead of me. Tawny noticed that earlier that day, there were lots of berries on the holly plants. When she ran downstairs to let in the paramedics, a lot of the berries were gone. She didn't tell her parents her suspicions, but she did tip off the paramedics so they had an idea about what might be making her ill."

"But they haven't confirmed it for sure yet?"

"No, or if they have, they haven't told Tawny. I don't know. It's a huge mess, and Tawny's a wreck. Tawny told me that Sabine had a couple of terrible fights with her mother and her dad, one after the other. Sabine's been acting really off lately. I get the sense that there's something really awful that Tawny's not willing to share with me yet, so there's nothing to do except wait until she's ready to talk. And Tawny's not the only one who's a wreck. I was on the phone with Zita not long before you got here, and she can't stop crying."

"Poor kid. First all that stress on her family with Bertie being ghosted, and now this."

"Uh-huh. I had a word with the Godspeeds. Zita really wants to see Sabine. Tawny says that they're keeping her under observation tonight, but she might be ready for visitors tomorrow. I was thinking, I have the first two periods free tomorrow. If you don't have any plans, I'd love it if you'd come with me in the morning. We'll pick up Zita, take her to the hospital, and hopefully, we can provide a little moral support."

"Sounds like a great idea."

"Do you mind?"

"No. It's all part of the job. If I can help a student in crisis, it's my duty to do so." I was briefly interrupted by Toby bringing me a dish filled with crumbled brownies and chocolate pudding, and whipped cream, saying that she'd made it herself and hoped I enjoyed it. I did.

"By the way," Toby told me. "About what I told you in the car? I cracked. Mom asked me what I said to you, and I couldn't stop myself from spilling my guts. Turns out, she was way cooler about it than I thought she'd be."

"Frankly, I'd have preferred it if she waited until her senior year of college to date, but if she wants to have a little good clean fun, I'm not going to be one of *those* mothers," Nerissa quipped.

"So you two are good?"

"We're great." Toby smiled and hurried out of the room.

Turning my attention back to the Sabine case, I told Nerissa, "This may be just what I need for a distraction. I've been obsessing about this whole Bertie situation. I need to remember that there are other students who need my attention."

"Yeah, I've been worried about you."

"Why? I'm fine."

"Like hell you are. You've been missing meals—something I've never known you to do in all the years we've been acquainted. You've been oversleeping so much you're practically in a coma. And now you spent twenty-five percent of the day swimming, like you're training to do the backstroke across the English Channel."

I wanted to respond with a sharp criticism of the many times when Nerissa's gotten too emotionally invested in a tricky situation with one of her girls, but I held my tongue. It was annoying, but she was right. I pride myself on my skill with wordcraft, but at the time, the only phrase I could possibly muster to describe my mental state was "totally messed up." When you get consumed by a case, you should take a break, because you can't do your best work when the investigation becomes your whole world. I busied myself with scraping my plate clean, knowing that whatever happened with catching the identity thieves, nothing would bring Bertie back. Right now, there were a couple of living teenaged girls who were trapped in the depths of their own personal hell, and Nerissa and I had chosen to take on jobs where we'd look out for young people like them.

When I got my law degree, I figured I'd make plenty of money, but I doubted that I'd do much actual good in the world. When my career derailed, and I wound up working as a private detective, I made barely enough cash at first to keep from starving and freezing (not that Mrs. Zwidecker would ever have kicked me out or stopped feeding me even if I was flat broke), and I wasn't sure most of the time whether I was helping people or unintentionally hurting them. Looking back at those two stages of my working life, I really didn't care for either profession at that time.

But now, as the Cuthbertson Student Advocate, I get a level of job satisfaction that I'd never before dreamed possible. After I confirmed the plans for tomorrow and kissed Nerissa good night, as I walked back to my car, I realized that even though my current job provided me with a decent living, it allowed me to go to bed with an easy conscience, knowing that I was doing my best to right some truly appalling situations. Moreover, being the Student Advocate gives me more than the ability to sleep well at night.

It gives me a reason to get up in the morning.

Chapter Six

The Night That Changed Everything

As it turns out, our plans for Monday morning were a bit different from how Nerissa had scheduled them the previous night. Sabine's mother checked her out of the hospital first thing in the morning, and though it took a considerable amount of begging and bawling on Zita's part to get Sabine's mother to agree, eventually, she capitulated and allowed Zita to come talk to her at their home. Since Sabine and Tawny's house was just a stone's throw down the road from Cuthbertson, we arrived at school as we normally did, quickly met up with Zita, and drove her to her friend's home. As we climbed out of my car, I noticed that some leaves from a holly plant were sticking out of the garbage can.

Luckily, it was Tawny who answered the door, having taken the day off of school to look after her sister. I was relieved, as I wasn't sure if her mother would have allowed Nerissa and me inside the house. I didn't know the woman well, but I'd recently offered Tawny some advice on how to look out for her own best interests while her parents' divorce was getting fouler and fiercer with each passing week. Tawny's mother never saw me or spoke to me, but when Tawny let it slip that she'd been coming to me for help, her mom threw a hissy fit. According to Tawny, some cushions had been thrown in her general direction. After a sustained period of screeching, Tawny capitulated, and told me the next day that she was grateful for my help, but she would no longer be coming to me for legal and tactical advice on how to stand up for her own interests during the divorce. This happens a lot. When divorcing parents—and their lawyers—hear that I'm assisting a kid, they tend to freak out and demand that the child remain defenseless and devoid of allies. Way too often, the kids capitulate, abandon the chance at self-preservation they are entitled to, and leave themselves to the mercy of a system that cares less about their rights than it does for any accused rapist or serial killer.

After the initial greeting, I asked Tawny where her mother was.

"Mom's meeting with her lawyer over coffee, and *that man*—" this was Tawny's preferred moniker for her mother's boyfriend—"is at work. We should have at least a half-hour before she gets back. Maybe a little more."

"Good." We heard the television droning from the living room and followed the noise of a panel of women talking about subjects of absolutely no interest to me whatsoever. Sabine was there, sprawled out on the sofa with a small hill of pillows under her head and so many fluffy blankets thrown over her it reminded me of "The Princess and the Pea" in reverse, with all the soft bedding on top of her rather than underneath.

Zita sprinted ahead of the two of us, jumped on top of the pile of blankets, and hugged her friend. They started chatting and crying, and without having to speak a word, the rest of us decided it was best to leave them alone for a little bit.

A little soft bawling filled the room, and Tawny crossed over to a small play-pen and lifted her daughter Rhiannon out, and bounced her up and down in her arms. "How's she doing?" Nerissa inquired.

"Great! She's a happy baby, isn't she? Yes, you are! You certainly are!" Tawny cooed. "She's the only person in this house who smiles all the time," she continued in her regular voice.

"That's something, at least." The conversation centered around baby Rhiannon for a while, until Nerissa lowered her voice and redirected the topic back to Sabine.

"So, is she going to be all right?"

"Yes. It turns out she didn't take enough of those berries to cause any serious problems. It just made her a little sick, and they pumped her stomach, and she was fine. It was the glass of brandy she took from the liquor cabinet that really made her ill."

"You know this for a fact? She deliberately ate those holly berries?" I felt a chill all over my body.

"Uh-huh."

"She admitted it?"

"As soon as she woke up, she broke into tears and told me exactly what she did. She was just so desperate, she wanted it all to end."

"Is she going to talk to somebody?"

"She didn't admit it to the doctors, just to me, and I didn't confirm it to them. She threw up the berries before they could be digested, and as far as my mom's concerned, Sabine snuck a little drink and couldn't hold it down. That's all, that's the end of it."

"Sabine needs to talk to somebody," Nerissa groaned. "I'll talk with my grandmother, she'll set up a meeting, and if Sabine wants to talk to someone else, she'll refer her to someone else." Cutherbertson Hall is very much a family affair for the Kaimings, with four generations of them working there in various capacities at one point or another. Keith's mother is the school psychologist.

Tawny nodded. "Dr. Kaiming's a great guidance counselor. I've visited her a bunch of times to vent about the divorce and childrearing. I'm sure she can help Sabine. I don't think she seriously wanted to die. I'm pretty sure this was just a cry for attention."

"I don't want to alarm you, Tawny, but don't take this too lightly. Just because she said that she's fine doesn't mean that she is. I won't relax until she talks with a professional. In fact..." Nerissa pulled out her phone. "I'm calling Grandma. I think she'll be willing to make a house call."

As Nerissa crossed into the corner to make her call, I kept my voice low as I continued to talk to Tawny. "I heard that Sabine had a major fight with both of your parents yesterday."

It was like watching a storm cloud settle over Tawny's face. "Yeah..."

"Do you want to tell me the whole story?"

She hesitated. "Can we wait a minute, please? I want to tell you and Miss

Kaiming both at once."

That was a reasonable request, and a minute later, when Nerissa was finished with her call, we were all perched on a pair of padded window seats in the corner. "Yesterday afternoon Sabine came across a report that was in Mom's purse. It was a DNA test her lawyer asked her to get."

"Who's her lawyer?"

"Michelle Lilith."

I shook involuntarily. Tawny looked surprised by my spasm, and Nerissa put a steadying hand on my knee. She knew hearing that woman's name had that sort of effect on me.

"Do you know Ms. Lilith?" Tawny asked.

"Yes. We have a long history." I paused, debating whether or not I should provide additional details, and contenting myself with adding, "I have first-hand experience seeing her at work on a divorce case."

"Oh. Which of your parents did she represent?"

"Can we please not talk about that woman right now? I just don't care to think about her any more than necessary."

"Sure, I get it. I don't care for her, either. Where was I?"

"The DNA test." I could see where this was going, and it made my stomach lurch.

"That's right. Well, without telling us, Mom took hairs from both my brush and Sabine's brush and sent them in for testing, along with a sample from Dad she took without his knowing. I don't know how she got it."

"It doesn't matter. An empty drink bottle, a licked envelope, a stolen comb or toothbrush...it's easy to get DNA if you're so inclined."

"Well, the long and the short of it is, I'm Dad's daughter, but Sabine... isn't. Apparently, Mom and her boyfriend have been having a relationship for way longer than we thought, and..." Tawny cradled her daughter to her chest and rocked her softly. "You can imagine how Sabine responded when she learned that."

"Are you talking about me?" We all jumped a bit as we turned and saw Sabine and Zita standing in the doorway.

Prevarication would have been a stupid waste of time. I looked Sabine right in the eyes. "Yes. Yes, we are. Would you like us to include you in our conversation now?"

Sabine took a minute to mull it over and finally replied, "Sure. Why not?"

"Good. Can we go into the living room? These benches aren't very comfortable."

A moment later, we were all settled in more posterior-friendly furniture. "So you know about the DNA test?" Sabine asked.

"Yes."

"Did you hear the details about my fight with Mom, and then with Dad—or not really my Dad…."

When Sabine showed no signs of finishing that sentence, I jumped in and explained, "Not the details. Just the general outline of the impetus for the arguments."

"Oh. Well, I confronted Mom, and she yelled at me for a long time about going through her purse. I was just looking for a tampon…I yelled back…And then I called Dad and asked him to come over, and I asked if he knew…I've made a mess of everything." She started sobbing. I picked up a box of tissues and pressed them into her hands, and Zita and Tawny slipped their arms around her.

"Would you like something to drink?" Nerissa asked.

After a few more sobs, Sabine requested a glass of ice water, and Nerissa went to the kitchen and returned with the desired beverage. We sat quietly as Sabine sipped and restored her composure. Eventually, she muttered. "You can imagine what I'm going through right now."

"I don't have to imagine," I replied. "I lived it."

"Seriously?" "Really?" "Are you kidding me?" Tawny, Sabine, and Zita all spoke simultaneously.

"Yep. I was in third grade, and shortly after my parents announced their divorce, my mother let a certain bit of information slip. Shortly afterwards, he took me and my brother to the doctor's for a blood test—he told us it was for cholesterol levels—and a bit later, once the results were in, he delivered a very…terse, extremely angry monologue to me, explained the results of the test, and made it clear that as far as he was concerned, there was no longer any bond of genes or affection that tied him to me, and from now on I was never to address him as "Dad" again, and from that moment on, I was essentially dead to him."

"Did he use those words?"

"Most of them. I cleaned his language up for your benefit." I took a breath and tried to smother the resurfacing angry memories that were making every muscle in my body clench. "Did the man you've always believed was your father respond in a similar manner?"

"No. He was angry, totally livid, but he wasn't angry at *me*. He started screaming about Mom, saying it must be some kind of trick, that she was trying to hurt him…I've never seen him like that. His face was the color of a plum. I thought he was going have a coronary. But he never focused his anger towards me."

I leaned back in my chair. "That's good, actually. That's a rather hopeful sign. At least, I hope it is."

Sabine drank some more water. "What really hurts me is that Mom's boyfriend… that turd…he's…." She shuddered, and a few drops of water splashed out of the glass and onto her shirt. "I can't take it." After daubing her eyes with a fresh tissue, she looked up at me. "What's your relationship with your biological dad like?"

"I've no idea who he is. Neither does my mother. She fought with my supposed father while they were dating, she went out, got drunk, met a man she remembers nothing about, and when she got her test results back, she decided she would keep me, but since she didn't think she could raise me alone, she convinced my not-father he was responsible and that he was duty-bound to give her a ring." I realized long ago that not only was it unlikely that I'd ever track my biological father down, but that the revelation that he had a heretofore unknown son could quite probably be an unpleasant shock for him. I already had an unbearably traumatic exchange when one man responded to not being my father. I don't want to take the risk of a second parallel outburst when a stranger finds out he contributed half of my DNA.

That's not to say I don't wonder about what that mystery sperm donor out there is like. I speculate all the time, extracting the bits of my personality that mirror strong traits in my mother and grandparents, and I wonder if the unmatched characteristics come from my biological father. I also wonder what he looks like, and what ethnicity he is. I haven't described myself physically much in this manuscript yet, but all I'll say here is that people often ask me what I am, exactly. My appearance, ethnically speaking, is best described as "ambiguous." I get a lot of people asking me, "Do you have Native American blood in you?" When I'm with the Kaiming family, most of whom are of half-Chinese and half-European heritage, some other guests sometimes ask me if I'm part-Asian too. I've also had lots of people ask me if I'm Jewish, or part Hispanic, and one very friendly man from Beirut once wanted to know if I was Lebanese. For many years, my standard response has been, "Your guess is as good as mine," and I swiftly and firmly change the subject and refuse to return to the topic. I suppose I could take one of those tests that give you your ethnic background, but I'm deeply suspicious of massive databases that keep track of lots of people's DNA. Unlike finding the person who ghosted Bertie, I can live quite happily without solving the mystery of finding my father's identity.

Sabine moaned for a while about being sired by a man she despised, and Tawny made it very clear that she was never, ever to put the qualifier "half" before referring to her as her sister. That comment seemed to have a placating effect on Sabine.

"I can't believe I did what I did yesterday. I didn't want to die. I don't want to kill myself. I just wanted to scare Mom and Dad, I wanted to make them realize what this was doing to me... and I thought if I could get them good and worried, everything would somehow be all right again. So I picked a handful of those holly berries and poured myself a glass of Mom's brandy, and the next thing I know, I'm waking up in the hospital." She cradled her head in her hands. "You've never been in that dark a place, have you?"

"When I was thirteen, I had a huge fight with my birth mother, and she said some very cruel things," Nerissa sighed. "Tawny knows the whole story. I didn't want to hurt myself, but I wanted to hurt her, so I met up with a friend of mine who was also in the middle of a fractious clash with his parents, and after two awkward, stupid, foolhardy minutes, that's how I got my daughter."

"That's a lot like how it happened with me. Only I was sixteen," Tawny added.

I wanted to tell Sabine that I'd been in that same dark place that she'd been yesterday, but I was suddenly totally emotionally exhausted, and I didn't have the strength to share at that point. At that point in my life, I'd never even told Nerissa this story, and it was something that was more appropriately told in private.

Around seventh grade, I started having some very bleak thoughts. It started around Christmas, when I'd made the mistake of wearing a watch my not-grandfather had given me when I was in the second grade, right before he passed away. It was a thin but handsome gold wristwatch, and my not-grandfather wanted to give it to the boy he thought was his eldest grandson. It was too valuable and delicate to wear every day, so I took it out only for special occasions. When my not-father stopped by in the middle of a family Christmas party to pick up my half-brother (I have no problem with qualifying my demi-sibling like that, as he's made it clear he has no interest in maintaining any sort of connection with me), he saw the watch on my wrist, flushed crimson, wrestled the watch from my wrist without a word, and gave it to my half-brother, whispering to him, "This should be yours. You're the real eldest grandson." I could have made a fuss. I certainly wanted to, but for reasons I can't understand, I stayed silent. My grandparents on my mother's side saw the whole thing, and later that evening, my grandfather took his wristwatch off and put it on me. He didn't say anything—he was the kind of man who never spoke if he could help it, but he didn't have to use words. This was a much larger watch than the one my not-grandfather gave me, with a stainless-steel band, and a 1936 "Walking Liberty" dollar coin as the face. It's never gained or lost any time, and aside from a clasp that usually takes three or four tries to unlatch, it's a great timepiece. That watch I started wearing every day.

I still can't bring myself to describe the events of the next few months in depth. As I mentioned earlier, my home situation fell apart. My wicked stepfather falsely accused me of something iniquitous he'd done himself, my half-brother confirmed the allegation for reasons I still don't understand,

and my mother believed them. The next thing I knew, I was a pariah in the house, and there was talk of shipping me off to a boarding school for children with "issues." I was still twelve, and I didn't know how to process everything or even put it into words, so I felt like I was drowning a thousand miles from shore.

When you're a kid, you know you're in trouble, but you often don't know how to help yourself, and at that age, an unquestionably unjust and challenging situation magnifies beyond all proportion to become totally hopeless. If I'd had someone to turn to, an adult I knew I could trust, someone who was fiercely and protectively on my side, my mental state would've been very different. There's a big difference between being caught in a struggle that you know will be a challenge to overcome and having an ally and being trapped in an impossible quagmire by yourself. That personal experience is yet another reason why I'm so passionate about my job.

At that time, even though I had a really good relationship with my maternal grandparents and uncle, I didn't see them all that much as my mother made a point of minimizing contact with them. I didn't feel like I could confide in them because in a serious lapse in judgment on my part, I didn't think they'd believe me either. I felt like I was completely on my own. I should have turned to Mrs. Zwidecker or another teacher, but due to my home situation, my faith in adults was completely shattered. In my defense, the same problem afflicts a lot of kids in comparable situations. I was sure that if I told anybody at all, no one would credit my story. They'd listen to my wretched stepfather explain everything away in his calm, reasonable, lying voice, and they'd watch my half-brother cry and parrot the lines he'd been fed, and they would unhesitatingly accept the premise that I was a little monster.

A couple of months passed, and despite my best efforts, I could see no way out of the situation except for one drastic, final solution. Eventually, I couldn't take another day of being confined to my room every hour I was home, taking my meals alone at my bedside end table. The other three members of the household were giving me the silent treatment. During the car rides to and from school, my mother would glance at me occasionally with fear and apprehension in her eyes, and when I left my bedroom to use the bathroom, I'd often catch my putrid stepfather leering at me across the house with a triumphant smirk. And as for my half-brother… he avoided me and kept his head studiously covered by a comic book in the car, and despite weeks of trying, I never got the chance to look at his face to glean some hint of why he had betrayed me.

So if you can't win, twelve-year-old me reasoned, why not give up and end the torture? During the first week of March, I started to make my plans. I thought of various options and dismissed some as too painful, others as too messy. Finally, I came up with an acceptable "exit strategy," as I euphemistically called it, and decided not to subject myself to another day of agony.

During my study hall at the end of the day, I wrote out a note. It was a long one, seven full pages, both front and back, and I managed to explain the whole situation in it, recounting my satanic stepfather's lies, my mother's refusal to listen to me and hear the truth, my half-brother's complicity, and my not-father's loathing for me. I didn't explain my plans for myself. I only stated that there'd be no point in looking for me, that I'd never be found. After school ended for the day, I stapled the note together, tucked it in my assignment notebook, and met up with Bertie at his locker. I didn't say much to him, just this:

ME. Bertie, you've been the best friend I could have possibly wanted.

BERTIE. You're welcome, Isaiah. I'm glad you're my friend, too.

ME. Here. (*I took off my grandfather's watch.*) My grandfather on my Mom's side gave me this at Christmas. I want you to have it.

BERTIE. I can't take it. It means too much to you.

ME. I don't need it anymore, Bertie. Just wear it and remember me.

And with that, I turned away and was enveloped in the crowd of students eager to rush home. I made my way to my locker, tossed my books inside, and left my note on the top shelf. Pulling on my heavy coat, I gently shut my locker and spun the dial. I hurried down to the after-school store and bought a couple of cookies—they were freshly baked and filled with rich chunks of chocolate that were firm on the outside, but oozing with molten gooey goodness on the inside. I decided to eat one right away while it was still warm, and then wrapped the other in a napkin and tucked it in my coat pocket.

Normally, I would have marched out the main door of the Middle School, where one of our neighbors whose kids also went to Cuthbertson would have picked me and my brother up, but that afternoon I slipped out one of the back doors, marched through the teacher's parking lot, and followed the footpath through the woods surrounding the school. Ten minutes later, I was close to a main road, and I walked northward for about six blocks until I reached a bus stop. I plonked myself on the bench and had a six-minute wait until the bus took me a couple of miles northward.

I'd chosen my last stop with great care. I was going to go to a park that I used to visit all the time with my family when I was little. We went there for picnics in the summer and snowshoeing in the winter. I hadn't been there since the third grade when my mother and the man I thought was my father took us there to eat hamburgers and play catch and fly a kite. A large black dog came running up to us midway through the afternoon, and with his well-groomed fur and collar, we knew he wasn't a stray, though his owner was nowhere to be found. My half-brother and I found a stick and played fetch with him for a while, before he went bounding away through the trees. Looking back, I now remember that both of my parents—or rather, one parent and one not-parent, though he didn't know it then—seemed distracted the whole time, and they were shooting each other odd looks every few minutes. In the months to come, I came to realize the excursion for what it was. They both knew that the divorce was coming. They just wanted to give their kids one last day as a family, before everything changed forever. A half-hearted attempt to provide a happy afternoon before the extended period of conflict and venom took over every aspect of our lives.

Four years later, that park had taken on a romanticized emotional resonance in my mind. It was a place of innocence and happiness, and countless times since my parents' split, I told myself that if only we'd gone there more often and had a bunch of additional joyful times there, my parents would have decided they were better off together and everything would have been all right. Of course, this wasn't true—I always knew this deep in my soul—but I found the thought very comforting, even if it was a pipe dream.

Walking to the park, I found it was much the same as the last time I'd been there, with a few significant changes. The trees seemed much taller, though they were bare. Most of the ground was still covered in snow, though here and there, a small patch of withered tan grass was exposed. A children's playground filled with rusted metal poles and splintering wooden planks was gone and had been replaced with a new, plastic structure. Even though I was much older than the intended user for this, I jumped onto a swing and started pumping myself back and forth, laughing and nearly forgetting the reason why I'd come to the park in the first place.

Eventually, I got too dizzy to continue swinging, and I staggered off and tramped eastward through the few remaining inches of snow towards the end of the park. When we'd visited in the past, my mother had made sure we stayed at least ten yards away from the edge of the park at all times. The park was located on a tall bluff overlooking Lake Michigan, and from the top of the cliff down to the frigid waters below was an approximately sixty-foot drop. A row of large boulders had been placed along the edge to form a very insecure barrier, and as I made my way to the edge, I saw that the thin strip of rocky beach was covered with large chunks of ice that had washed ashore after breaking off the surface of the thawing lake.

I stood at the edge, looking downwards and trying to prepare myself for what I had come there to do. Just as I was steeling my nerve, I remembered the cookie in my pocket. I wasn't about to let it go to waste, so I sat down on the flattest of the boulders, unwrapped my cookie, and started eating it slowly, turning each bite over and over with my tongue and allowing the soft chocolate to cover every last little bit of my mouth. That was probably the longest I'd ever taken to eat a cookie. By the time I'd swallowed the last crumb and licked my fingers clean, the sun had set, and the sky was rapidly darkening.

I was just about to stand up when I heard a little jingling noise to my left, and as I turned, I saw an old friend running towards me. It was the dog I'd played with over four years earlier. I didn't know if he recognized me or if he was just naturally friendly, but he came straight up to me and put his head in my lap. I stroked him, patting his head and running my hand along his back. His fur was incredibly soft and silky, and when I checked the tag on his collar, I learned his name was Sandalphon.

From time to time, I gently informed him that it was nice spending time with him, but he needed to head home. Like many dogs, he was uninterested in taking orders, and he only nestled closer to me, putting a paw on my knee and making it impossible for me to stand.

Having no watch, I had no idea how long he was there, but without sunlight, the cliff was getting blustery, and the wind was growing in strength. Sandalphon's body heat kept me warm, though. The last of the blue had faded from the sky, and hundreds of stars started twinkling above me.

The stillness was shattered by a "Woof! Woof! Woof! Woof! Woof!" from Sandalphon. I wondered what was making him bark, and then I heard a familiar voice saying, "Isaiah! Is that you?"

I turned and saw Bertie sprinting across the field towards me, calling, "He's here! He's here! He's okay!"

Bertie was more accurate than he knew. Because for the first time in many months, I had the vague but hopeful feeling that I would be okay in every sense of the word.

The next thing I knew, Mr. Godspeed was there, asking me if I was all right, and once I assured him that I was, he helped me up and started hurrying me to the car. I vaguely remember Sandalphon rushing away into the night, and Mrs. Godspeed started peppering me with one question after another.

I should point out that this incident took place well before cell phones became ubiquitous. Some people had car phones that plugged into the car's cigarette lighter portal (yes, those were a thing when I was in Middle School, too), but many of these car phones had iffy reception, so if you were away from home and needed to make a call, most people had to find a public pay phone. The Godspeeds didn't have a car phone, so that's exactly what they had to do.

A couple of minutes later, we stopped at a small pizza parlor I'd never visited before, and Mr. Godspeed pulled a handful of change out of his pocket and started making calls. Mrs. Godspeed settled Bertie and me into a booth in the corner, ordered us some food and drinks, and hurried over to the pay phone next to the one her husband was using in order to make some calls herself.

Bertie started filling me in on what had happened. I'd scared the living phlegm out of him by what I'd said to him (not his words), and as soon as he'd lost sight of me in the crowd, he'd gone straight to the teacher at Cuthbertson he trusted most: Mrs. Zwidecker. I don't know why I'd never considered confiding in her. I should have. She also became worried as soon as she heard the story, and after a quick and unsuccessful look around to find me, she summoned a custodian to let her into my locker. She found the note I'd written right away, and after a rapid read-through, she launched into five-alarm emergency mode.

Within minutes, she was on the P.A. system summoning all the remaining teachers at school to her classroom. She must've made the announcement right after I left the building. Once the faculty was on red alert, Mrs. Zwidecker, who knew my grandparents from church, called them, and they called my uncle to help with the search. I'd left no clues about where I was going in my note, so most of the teachers and my relatives started driving around in different directions looking for me, after the school secretary made a couple of dozen copies of a picture of me from the most recent yearbook. Mrs. Zwidecker and the school secretary manned the phones at Cuthbertson, after advising everybody to find a phone and check in every fifteen minutes. It was not the most efficient or organized operation, especially considering that everybody called in at the same time, leading to lengthy, time-wasting busy signals. Still, all the parties involved deserved an "A" for effort, and I should point out that since I started working for the school, I helped institute a much more streamlined emergency plan for the eventuality that anything like that ever happened again, using contemporary technology. Thank God, we haven't needed to use it yet.

Over the next twenty minutes, the pizzeria started filling up with Cuthbertson teachers and staff, my grandparents, and my uncle. I knew most of the teachers, all of whom seemed genuinely concerned about me. At the time,

Keith was still in grad school and was still just over a year from teaching at Cuthbertson himself, but he'd joined in the effort as well, riding around with his grandfather, who also teaches history. This was the first time I'd ever met him, and I had no idea that at some point in the future, he'd become my father-in-law. Funny how life connects you to people in unexpected ways.

For a day that had begun so hopelessly, the evening wrapped up quite nicely. Several teachers stopped by for a slice of pizza, but for most of the night, it was just me, the Godspeeds, my grandparents, and my uncle. At some point, Mrs. Zwidecker informed me that she'd left a message at my mother's workplace to let her know I was missing, and that she'd left a second message to inform her that I'd been found, but even though she'd asked her to call her at the pizza parlor, the hours passed with no word from her.

Eventually, the relieved and joyous atmosphere faded a little, and by the time we'd all eaten our fill, everybody was ready to be a bit more serious again, and it was time for a somber conversation about me and what I'd planned to do. I tried to assure everybody that the dark moment had passed, and no matter what happened, I'd never go down that bleak road again. Everybody seemed glad to hear that, but my family members were wise enough to realize that nothing would get better unless some drastic changes happened.

My grandparents informed me that from that point onwards, I would be living with them, and my uncle got in touch with some friends of his in the police department. In two days' time, all of my belongings had been transferred to my grandparents' house, and in less than two weeks, my stepfather had fled, taking away as many personal possessions as would fit into a set of suitcases, cleaning out the bank accounts he'd shared with my mother, and vanishing into the night, leaving behind enough evidence in a forgotten lockbox in the back of his closet to not only clear my name, but to finally convince my mother that I'd been telling the truth by revealing what he'd done to my half-brother and other little boys. Somehow, it wasn't enough to compel her to apologize or invite me back into her house. By that point, it didn't really matter to me. My half-brother started seeing a psychiatrist, and I began counseling sessions with my uncle.

The memories of that pivotal day half a lifetime ago whirled around my mind as I wrestled with the prospect of telling everybody in the room the story. I thought maybe it would help Sabine, yet those actions were such a source of shame to me that it physically hurt me to remember myself at my lowest and darkest. In the end, I stayed silent, as Nerissa led the conversation, providing emotional support to the sisters, until her grandmother arrived, ready to talk to Sabine.

Before they could get a chance to converse, another pair of cars pulled into the driveway, and Sabine and Tawny's mother entered the house along with her lawyer, Ms. Lilith.

"What the hell are you doing in my house?" Tawny and Sabine's mother demanded to know.

Nerissa managed to form one-sixteenth of a syllable before the woman, who I was disliking more and more with each word that spewed forth from her sour mouth, interrupted her. "It doesn't matter. All of you out. Now!"

Dr. Geraldine Kaiming was unflappable. "I have been informed that your daughter Sabine may have attempted to harm herself, and I was called to talk to her. I have a duty of care–"

"My daughter's fine. Out! Now!"

"I am staying, and I will speak to—"

"No, you won't!"

Ms. Lilith put a hand on her client's shoulder. "Are you telling me that you haven't had Sabine talk to a mental health professional yet?"

"She's perfectly fine! She's just a little drama queen, that's all."

Fixing her client with a steely glare, Ms. Lilith spoke softly but clearly. "It is my professional advice that you allow Dr. Kaiming to interview your daughter immediately." She whispered in Tawny and Sabine's mother's ear for about a minute, and eventually convinced her client of the wisdom of taking all the steps possible to prevent her daughter from doing harm to herself again.

"Fine," the woman who wasn't close to making the list of the top 50,000 mothers of the year in Milwaukee snarled. "The shrink can stay. But the rest of them have thirty seconds to leave. I'll get you those papers you wanted." With that, she stomped upstairs.

Nerissa rose to leave. "Thank you," she said to Ms. Lilith.

"You're welcome. Contrary to Isaiah's belief, I am not a monster who cares nothing for children. Sabine, I hope that you are feeling better, and I hope that your talk with Dr. Kaiming goes well."

Nerissa hugged her grandmother and the sisters while Zita pulled on her coat.

"I know this divorce situation is getting worse," I told the sisters. "Please talk to me if—"

"I want to, but I made my mom a promise, and I can't break it," Tawny groaned. "I swore to her I wouldn't come to you for help with fighting the divorce, and I just can't–"

"I get it, Tawny. You gave your word, and even if you made it under duress, you feel honor-bound to keep it. But to the best of my knowledge, Sabine didn't make that promise."

Upon hearing that little loophole, both sisters smiled for the first time that morning.

"And you didn't pledge to your mother that you wouldn't come to *me* for help, did you? Nerissa added with a grin of her own.

"You didn't hear any of that," I informed Ms. Lilith as we passed by her on our way out.

"Do you really think that I don't care about those girls?"

"I've seen you at work. If you really cared about kids, you'd specialize in another field of law."

"You are so bitter towards me."

"Maybe that's—"

Nerissa put a hand on my shoulder. "That's enough, Funderburke. Please. Don't start an argument. For me, please?"

When she put it like that, I couldn't deny her request for me to be on my best behavior. I gave the obliterator of families and extractor of funds a curt nod, wished the girls the best, and soon Nerissa, Zita, and I were on the way back to Cuthbertson.

"I want to thank you for being there for my parents," Zita told us once we'd arrived.

"Your family has been there for me during the worst times of my life. It's my pleasure and my duty to support them, anyway I can," I replied.

"I almost forgot." Zita pulled a wrapped package out of her backpack and handed it to me.

Tearing off the paper, I discovered a framed photograph of Bertie and me. It was taken that fateful night at the pizza parlor. I suddenly realized that I didn't have any pictures of the two of us, aside from a few group shots with other students in yearbooks. I grew up in the time before young people took more selfies than they do deep breaths, when snapshots were saved for special occasions and parties. I don't know why Mrs. Godspeed took that photo that night, but I was very glad she did.

"She found it in a shoebox the other night," Zita explained. "You know, she put away all of her pictures of Bertie after he died. It was too hard for her to look at them. Now, with everything going on, she thinks she's ready to bring his photos back out again. She's not quite ready to put them around the house yet, but she's looking at them several times a day. She found this and knew she had to make you a copy."

I ran the back of my hand over my eyes. "Thank you. Tell her—no, I'll call her tonight and thank her myself."

Zita pointed at the picture. "Bertie's wearing your watch in that picture."

My eyes moved from the photograph to my grandfather's watch on my wrist. "Yes, he is."

"Why?"

"I lent it to him to thank him for being such a good friend to me."

That was true, but Nerissa could tell from my voice that I was holding something back. She shot me a look, making it clear that she didn't expect me to unburden myself in front of Zita, but she did expect me to tell her the whole story at the earliest possible opportunity.

That night, Bertie had tried to give the watch back, but I'd told him to hang on to it. He said he couldn't keep it, so I told him to borrow it for a little while. I couldn't think of an adequate way to show my gratitude at that moment, so why didn't he just hang onto it, at least for a few weeks, and every time he wore it, he could think of how he'd saved me.

Bertie wore that watch like a badge of honor. I promised myself I'd never ask for it back, and I didn't. Mr. Godspeed returned it to me without my asking for it after the authorities returned Bertie's personal effects to them.

I looked down at the photo of Bertie and me, and once again, my mind flashed back to that pivotal night, where I had begun the day devoid of courage and without any strength, only to reach the end of the day with a renewed sense of optimism that maybe my future wasn't as bleak and hopeless as I'd come to believe. Realizing that there were people in my life who cared about me deeply made all the difference. Scrutinizing Bertie's face in the picture, I was reminded of just how huge an impact he had made in my life. Having him for a friend had given me the will to live, and that night, for the first time in a long while, a long stream of tomorrows seemed like a blessing rather than a curse.

Two weeks after that photograph was taken, Bertie was murdered.

Chapter Seven

The Trap is Set

I had expected my schedule to be fairly clear that day, but just as I was getting out of the car, I received a text telling me that I needed to rush over to the Middle School as soon as I could, as the fifth-grade math teacher had taken ill and they needed me to substitute for her. I informed Nerissa of this as Zita ran ahead of us into the building, and Nerissa nodded, pecked me on the cheek, and whispered, "We'll talk more later." There wasn't any anger in her tone. From the look on her face, her mind was full of concern and curiosity. She knew I was holding something back from her, and she wanted to give me time to process and prepare, but she believed that a few hours at most would be sufficient.

I made my way to the math classroom, and the French teacher, who had the period off, looked relieved at no longer having to proctor the students, who were practically bouncing out of their chairs. I wasn't expecting the reception I got, but a room full of wide smiles, and a deafening "MR. FUNDERBURKE!" assured me that they weren't out for blood.

When the students have enthusiasm for something, you might as well let them run with it, as long as you can find a way to eventually tie it back into what you're supposed to be teaching. I was still wearing my walking coat, and when three of the kids simultaneously asked where I got it, I told them the story of how, in the early years of my P.I. days, I cleared the name of a teenager who was falsely accused of murdering his father. I took care to bowdlerize the case for delicate young ears, but ten minutes later, by the time I reached the tale's conclusion, where the teen and his mother, having no money to pay for my services, gave me this coat, which his father had recently bought but never worn, in lieu of my usual fee. Given how often I wear it, and how much I love it, I came out ahead on the deal.

Realizing that the students hadn't interrupted me once, I decided to try to keep up the momentum by segueing into discussing some of my favorite lessons from when I was in Middle School math. As an example, I picked up a trio of plastic boxes that had rested on the top of the shelf in the corner of the classroom since before I was in fifth grade, preceding the tenure of the current math teacher. After asking to make sure that their regular instructor hadn't performed this demonstration before, and hoping that I wasn't spoiling a future lesson their regular teacher had planned, I set the three boxes down on the desk at the front of the room and asked them which was the largest by volume. The first was a cube ten inches to a side, the second was narrower but longer, and the third box was the longest and thinnest of them all.

The class was about evenly split on what they thought was the biggest box, and once the votes were in, I walked over to the little sink in the corner of the room meant to encourage frequent handwashing, and filled the first box up with water. With a bit of showmanship, I then poured the contents of the first box into the second, demonstrated to the class that they both contained exactly the same amount of water, and then repeated the process for the last box.

"You see?" I asked them. "Each box contains the same volume, but their proportions are different. Each has a different length, width, and depth, but when you multiply each box's measurements together, the result's the same. One thousand cubic centimeters. Some might look bigger or smaller at first glance, but just because something appears to be a certain way, that doesn't mean that it's your initial impression is accurate. You have to check your facts and be prepared to admit that your first thoughts were incorrect."

I extended the lesson through the use of some optical illusions I found on the Internet and projected on the screen at the front of the room, and tied it all into geometry. By the end of the class, I could say with absolute honesty that the kids had learned something from me.

Each of the day's remaining classes followed the same template. The kids asked for a story about one of my cases, and I tied it into a lecture on how thinking outside the box and never taking anything for granted before checking it out thoroughly yourself was crucial to being a successful private investigator, though I made sure not to ignore the math principles connected to the assigned topics for the day.

After the last students were dismissed for the day, I gathered up their turned-in homework assignments, tucked them into the regular teacher's mailbox in the Middle School faculty lounge, and made my way back to my office. I was riding the high of a successful day of teaching when I found Nerissa sprawled out in one of the chairs reserved for my guests. I swear, nobody can look more comfortable in a chair than Nerissa. She looked as if that cheap old lump of vinyl was a cloud that had been freshly warmed by the posterior of an angel.

Shutting and locking the door, I sat in the matching chair next to her, and if my inner thoughts were reflected through my posture, it was obvious that I wasn't nearly as snug in my seating arrangement as she was.

I just looked at her for a moment, appreciating the full-length wine-colored sweater dress she was wearing, with a coat a lot like mine over it, though hers reached her ankles as opposed to my knees, and had a couple more buttons.

She gave me a little smile that wasn't quite reflected in her eyes and said, "So?"

I was all set to evade. I didn't want to relive those memories again that day. I made up my mind to tell her that I was sleepy from another poor night of sleep and that I was just a little slow.

Instead, when I opened my mouth, the entire story came pouring out, with no restraint. I did not plan to tell that story, I did not want to tell that story, but my tongue and vocal cords were no longer under my control. Much like when answering a call of nature, once I began, I couldn't stop until all of the nasty stuff was purged from me.

Finally, I reached the end of my narrative, and looked at Nerissa, apprehensive about what I'd see in her face when she knew the truth about the lowest point in my life. She moved her hands from where she had them clasped around her knees and said, "Stand up, please."

I obeyed as she rose simultaneously, and then wrapped her arms around me in the tightest hug I'd ever had in my life. I had hoped that her response would be along these lines, but I hadn't realized that I'd be so relieved by it. I reciprocated, and when she pulled away several minutes later, she started scrutinizing the front of her coat and mine to make sure that she hadn't gotten saltwater stains on them. That woman is obsessed with keeping her clothes pristine. I swear, if Nerissa ever gets shot, she's going to check all her clothing and treat it to make sure the bloodstains don't set in before she calls 911 for an ambulance.

She went through the better part of a box of tissues, and I'd be withholding information if I didn't admit to doing my part in helping to fill the wastebasket with damp paper. Eventually, emotional exhaustion or possibly dehydration set in, and we sank back into our chairs.

"I wish I'd gotten on that plane and moved to Milwaukee when I was six," she quipped. "It would have been nice to have known you a lot earlier."

"I wish you could've known Bertie. It would've helped me through the divorce so much, with the three of us together." I didn't add that I probably would've had a crush on her for an additional eight years. I wouldn't dignify my feelings towards her as love at first sight, but it was close. When I first got to know her about a month into our freshman year in English class, she had just discovered a loophole in the Cuthbertson dress code and was exploiting it for all it was worth. The rules clearly state that students have to wear a white dress shirt, dress shoes, a black blazer, and black pants. Girls have the option of wearing skirts that are knee-length or longer, and boys must wear ties. The rules clearly stated that the pants could not be made of denim, but as Nerissa would point out, whenever a teacher challenged her, there was nothing in the dress code that said that her uniform couldn't be made out of leather. I was smitten, and have remained so ever since. It wasn't just the outfit itself, though I freely admit to being a huge fan of it and all subsequent fashion choices of Nerissa's along those lines. It was her attitude. She was basically saying, "Look, I'm following your rules, but I'm following them *my way*. I may not be doing exactly what you had in mind, but you're the ones who drew up the regulations, and it's not my fault you left a loophole. By your own standards, I've done nothing wrong, so leave me alone." At the time, it wasn't so much cowardice that kept me from expressing my feelings to her so much as PTSD from being wrung through the divorce grinder and my mother's abhorrent second marriage. At the time, I couldn't see how any romantic relationship, no matter what the level, could possibly work out for the best, and even if one did take the leap, the potential consequences far outweighed the benefits. It took a long time for me to work my way through that mindset, but I'm very glad I did.

"Of course, if I'd moved to Milwaukee earlier, it would've changed the trajectory of my birth mother's life, too, and I'd never have been adopted by the Kaimings. Or had Toby. So my whole career would've been different, and all of my girls would be left on their own."

"Mm-hmm." I pondered the possibility that if Nerissa had been our pal in seventh grade, she might have arranged some sort of hangout on that fateful day, and Bertie would still be with us. I dropped that train of thought as soon as I could. Dwelling on all those "what if's?" can ruin your present.

We sat quietly for a bit before Nerissa broke the silence.

"So, want to get yogurt?"

"Sounds great to me."

* * *

The rest of the evening passed quietly. While Nerissa has to take her work home with her, with grading and class preparation and dissertation work, when the bell rings at the end of the day, my time is my own, unless there's something to investigate, like background checks on potential hires. After a swim that was much shorter than the previous day's, I ate dinner (Beef Stroganoff) with Mrs. Zwidecker, and spent the rest of the night organizing my case files, along with much too much time surfing the Internet.

The next morning, I learned that I'd have to substitute teach fifth-grade math again, which was fine with me, aside from the fact that I preferred the Upper School lunch (chicken enchiladas) to the Middle School lunch (turkey subs). Once I realized that I had a free period that coincided with one of the Upper School lunch times, I figured I'd wait until then to have my midday meal.

As it turned out, it was serendipitous that I'd decided to eat in the high school, as while I was stacking my dirty dishes in the kitchen turntable, I saw a pair of familiar figures talking to a couple of people from the Development Office. I wasn't sure whether I should say hello or not, but Vianne Coquina saw me, excused herself, and walked up to me. I don't think her husband even noticed she was gone, and he certainly didn't appear to be aware of my presence.

"Hello, Funderburke. How's everything for you today?"

"I'm taking a brief lunch break from Middle School substituting duties."

"Ugh. I don't envy you that."

"May I ask why?"

"Let's just say there's a good reason Tyler and I don't have kids. Other than the fact I'd have to let him touch me."

We were only five yards away from Tyler, and I didn't think that she'd dipped her voice quite enough to keep him from hearing. Despite my concerns, Tyler didn't seem to be aware of his wife revealing some unsettlingly personal details of their relationship. I must admit I was curious as to why she'd be so indiscreet, but it wouldn't do for there to be a scene in the corridor, so I changed the subject.

"I see you got to try our school lunch. What did you think, Vianne?"

"How did you know?"

"There's a little spot of red sauce on your chin." I leaned over, plucked a napkin from the dispenser, and handed it to her.

"I have to remember what your job is." Vianne laughed as she wiped her face. "It was excellent. Your lunches are much better than the ones at my old high school."

"Where did you go to high school?"

Perhaps she didn't hear me, because she responded by saying, "We came here today to consult with your Development Office for your annual fundraising auction. My husband knows a bunch of businesspeople who'd be willing to donate some merchandise, so they're pretty receptive to hearing some of his ideas. He's trying to finagle a spot as one of the auctioneers. It'll probably help him make even more connections."

"If he'd lived a couple of decades ago, he'd probably have the biggest Rolodex in town."

"Uh-huh. He's never made a friend in his life without first calculating how that acquaintanceship might enrich him or improve his position. I should have said, 'acted friendly towards someone.' He doesn't have any actual friends."

I wanted to ask what decision-making metrics went into his selection of her as his wife, but I kept my lips shut. I practically had to bite down upon my tongue to keep myself from inquiring what exactly was going through her head when she agreed to marry the unctuous little lecher.

Vianne gave me a little nod, indicating that she wanted me to step behind the partition extending from the wall, out of the sight of her husband and the members of the Development Office. "I was talking to the Godspeeds today about some ideas I had about how to make their new project more efficient."

"Oh? What are they?"

"I need a little time to work out a few details. I'll let you know when you come in to volunteer for the trial run for the meal deliveries."

"All right."

"I'm just worried about them. There's a haunted look in both of their eyes. It hasn't been there before, and it's unsettling."

"Because of the whole ghosting situation?"

"I think so. That's the only thing it could be, don't you think?"

I nodded. What else could affect them like that?

"They gave the police a call today, and the police were very noncommittal. They provided no details, but from their tone, the Godspeeds got the impression that the trail is cold and the police were on the verge of giving up, though of course, they wouldn't admit it."

"What about the letter I sent them?"

"They think that it was a prank played on you. The theory is it was a fake letter meant to get your goat. Who sent it, they don't know."

It was at that moment that I promised myself that I would personally see to it that the miscreant who had appropriated Bertie's name would see the inside of a prison cell.

Tyler's voice called out, "Vianne?" His tone was simultaneously beckoning and whiny.

"My husband calls." Vianne placed her hand on my shoulder for a fraction of a second. "Lovely talking to you, Funderburke. See you soon."

I rushed back to my office and pulled the burner phone out of my coat pocket. As I waited for it to turn on, I found myself bouncing up and down with impatience. After thirty seconds that felt like half an hour, I discovered that there were no text messages for me. I had mailed the letter at a box where it had been picked up in the late morning on Monday. It was possible that it would be delivered in Green Bay that day, but there was no way of knowing if the mailman had dropped it off in the P.O. Box already or if it wouldn't arrive until later in the afternoon. And there was no reason it wouldn't come until Wednesday or Thursday. No guarantee the recipient wouldn't pick it up until the next day. I could be waiting until Friday for a response, if I received one at all.

The rest of the day, I kept giving my students little projects to work on in small groups, so I could duck behind the file cabinets and check if the burner phone got any texts. With each negative response, I grew jumpier. I admit I was off my teaching game that afternoon because I was so distracted. Finally, with fifteen minutes remaining in the school day, I let out a whoop that caused eleven students to inquire about my well-being. I'd finally gotten a response. I realized I wasn't breathing as I read and reread the message, "CAN YOU MEET ME AT DELLTON'S AT 6 TODAY. PLEASE BRING THE MONEY. LET ME KNOW ASAP."

"Mr. Funderburke? Are you okay?"

"Absolutely spiffing," I assured the girl. "Perfectly peachy keen." I typed out, "I'LL BE THERE AT 6. SEE YOU SOON." as fast as I could. Despite the brevity of the message, I made five typos and had to go back and correct them. I sent the text, tried to restrain myself from doing a little dance, and reemerged from behind the file cabinets with a renewed bounce in my step. My mind may not have been focused on teaching math from lunchtime on, but I gave those kids a first-rate educational experience for the final quarter-hour of the day.

When class dismissed, I was out of there faster than any student. I broke the Cuthbertson Hall track team record for the 200-yard dash as I zoomed back to my office. A few feet away from the door, I nearly ran over Nerissa and Esme, but I brought myself to a halt just in time, though I suspect that I left skid marks on the floor.

"Way to put on the brakes, Funderburke," Nerissa laughed. "Esme stopped by to talk to the Cuthbertson food services team. We're going to see if we can donate our leftovers for the Meals on Wheels for children program."

"That's great," I said with my mind elsewhere.

"Something wrong?"

"No. Something's right." I explained everything, and as soon as I finished, Nerissa was as excited as I was.

"So, are we going on a road trip?" Nerissa squealed.

"Yes. Grab your coat and use the bathroom. If we leave in five minutes, even allowing for rush hour traffic, we should get there just in time."

"Aren't you going to call the police?" Esme asked.

"They've given up on the case. Anyway, the detectives assigned to the case are too far away to make it in time."

"I'll grab my things." Nerissa hurried away in a sparkling flash. She was wearing the metallic copper pantsuit she'd told me about a few days earlier. It wasn't the sort of clothing choice you'd normally make for sprinting, but it didn't seem to hinder Nerissa at all.

I was just about to hurry to the restroom when Esme tugged at my sleeve. "Can I come with you, please? I promise I won't get in the way. It's just that I've been obsessing about this, and…."

Smiling, I held up a reassuring hand to let her know she didn't need to justify her desire to be a part of this. "Of course, you can join us."

Ten minutes later, after we were all prepared, I'd called Mrs. Zwidecker and told her not to expect me for dinner, Nerissa had done the same with her family, we'd picked up some snacks from the after-school store, I'd looked up the best route to Dellton's, and I'd informed campus security that Esme's car would be parked in our lot for much of the evening, we climbed into my car and started heading northwards.

I felt my stomach breakdancing. Part of me was concerned that it could be dangerous, and part of me noted with grimness that if the identity thief acted up, he might have way more to fear from me than I did of him. I tried to reassure myself that it was more likely than not that an identity thief would be a non-violent criminal. I make no claims to being incredibly skilled in self-defense—my knowledge of martial arts is mostly limited to what I see in action movies and I'm better at avoiding confrontations than engaging in them—but I have some basic education in defensive techniques, and I've seen first-hand how Nerissa can take care of herself. I was a little more concerned about Esme. At just barely over five feet tall and possessing negligible width, I doubted she'd be of much help in a tense situation.

While Nerissa and Esme made small talk, I heard two different portions of my personality—Sensible Funderburke and Impulsive Funderburke duking it out in my head.

SENSIBLE FUNDERBURKE. Are you absolutely positive that you don't want to call the police?

IMPULSIVE FUNDERBURKE. They're can't drive up from Northern Illinois in time.

SENSIBLE FUNDERBURKE. What about the Green Bay Police?

IMPULSIVE FUNDERBURKE. What about them? They're busy with other problems. An identity thief isn't going to be high on their list of priorities. They don't know anything about the case anyway.

SENSIBLE FUNDERBURKE. You don't know that. You're just saying that because if you step aside and let the people who are trained for handling situations like this take charge, you'll lose the chance to do what you really want. You're determined to catch this guy yourself.

IMPULSIVE FUNDERBURKE. And what's wrong with that?

SENSIBLE FUNDERBURKE. What will you do if you catch him? What if he's part of a bigger criminal organization? What if his partners come after you? Or if they come after people you care about? Maybe even the Kaiming kids? Or what if something you do prevents him from revealing information about other identities he's stolen? Or what if the authorities get upset with you for interfering in an open case and take your private investigator license away?

IMPULSIVE FUNDERBURKE. Shut up.

SENSIBLE FUNDERBURKE. You know I'm right.

FUNDERBURKE FUNDERBURKE. Maybe you have a point, but right now, I'm going with Impulsive Funderburke. Sensible Funderburke, you sit tight and help me drive safely.

As I privately acknowledged that I was letting my personal desire for revenge against my late friend drive me and smother my concerns about safety and career repercussions, I was driven out of my reverie by Nerissa gently poking me on the shoulder.

"What?"

"Esme's been talking about how the Godspeeds have been really distracted ever since they found out about the ghosting, and I said that it's been affecting you, too."

"Yeah, it definitely has." I mentioned how I'd been swimming for way longer than I thought I had on Sunday.

"Wow. That's pretty impressive."

"Don't you mean *unsettling*?" I asked Esme. "I mean, losing all track of time like that?"

"I was thinking about the endurance it takes to swim that long. You must be in fantastic shape. I mean, you certainly look really fit." In the rearview mirror, I could see Esme's face suddenly flush with embarrassment. "Nerissa, please don't think I'm hitting on your man. I just...."

Nerissa laughed. "I know you, Esme. It's fine."

"Thanks. Well, anyway, you've completely trimmed down since you were a kid, Funderburke."

"Yeah, I had a growth spurt not long after Bertie died, and before I knew

110

it I was a twig." I tried to put a gentle edge in my tone to make it subtly but firmly clear that I didn't want to talk about that rather painful era of my adolescence.

Esme suddenly got very quiet. "I'm worried about that. The Godspeeds had really been healing from that whole ordeal, and now I'm afraid the wound is opening up again."

"Unfortunately, I'm sure you're right." I didn't want to add that I knew this to be true from personal experience. Upon glancing at Nerissa's face, I realized I didn't need to say it. It was blatantly obvious.

"You started volunteering with the Godspeeds right after you graduated from high school, right?" Nerissa asked.

"Actually, it was March of my senior year."

"High school or college?"

"High school. I couldn't afford to go…anyway, they were holding a party for local kids for the anniversary of the…you know. So I wandered in, thinking I'd just grab some free food, and then Mr. And Mrs. Godspeed started talking, and it touched something in me. Everything they were talking about, like looking out for children and providing help for anybody who needed it. It just struck a chord in me. I found myself wishing that they'd been around when I was younger. I didn't really know any of the other young people there, and right before I was about to leave Mrs. Godspeed came up to me and started talking, and after a minute, Mr. Godspeed joined us…they were so kind. They were the parents I'd always wished I had for myself. I found myself coming back, just for the chance to talk to them again. And then I kept returning, and I've been volunteering for them ever since."

After a pause, Nerissa, who was still embarrassed about asking whether Esme was referring to high school or college, asked. "Esme, I don't want to step somewhere you don't want me to tread, but I don't think you've ever mentioned your parents before."

"Yeah…that's because there's not much to tell. I never knew my father, and as for my mother…when I was six years old, she walked out of the apartment, and I never saw her again."

"Who raised you?" I asked, knowing immediately that I was veering into personal territory. I realized that I wasn't the only one who kept a lot of the darker details about my childhood private.

"I don't have any other relatives that I know of, so I was shuffled around a few foster homes. One was awful. The others were okay I was desperate to get away from the terrible one, but luckily a social worker realized what was going on there, and I got transferred to a pretty decent place. It was kind of crowded, but I was happy enough there until I turned eighteen." Esme shrugged. "Now I just want to help kids who remind me of me at that age."

For the previous Christmas, Nerissa's Great-Aunt Scholastica had given both of us plaques that said, "Be the person you needed when you were younger." We both put them on our office walls. I'm not much of one for motivational posters, but that little mantra appeals to me deeply.

We spent the next hour and a half swapping stories of rough times growing up, calling out people who were supposed to look out for us who let us down, and how we'd been lucky enough to discover people who came to our rescue.

There's no need for me to repeat our conversation. I've already shared much of what I told Esme and Nerissa that evening, and Nerissa would prefer that a lot of what she shared remain private for the time being.

The journey to Green Bay went swiftly, and by the time we reached the city limits, the light had completely faded from the sky, and even though I made a couple of wrong turns trying to find Dellton's, we got there at about a quarter to six. After a quick visit to the facilities, we gathered around a table near the front door, and I tried not to admit to myself that I didn't have a solid plan for how to proceed.

Dellton's was a pretty nice place, clean and comfortable-looking. When the waitress asked us what we wanted, I asked for a bowl of soup. That's a trick I learned from my mentor in the P.I. business. If you're waiting at a restaurant, soup is the quickest thing that can be served. If you can be called away at any moment, you don't want to be waiting around for an entrée you may never get to taste. Nerissa and Esme asked for salads, which I suppose is not too much less efficient, especially if the establishment pre-tears the lettuce. Our food and waters arrived within two minutes, and I insisted on paying right away, just in case we had to leave abruptly. The soup was chicken mushroom dumpling, and it tasted like it was made from scratch. Unfortunately, I couldn't really enjoy it like it deserved to be savored, as the anticipation was making my stomach do cartwheels.

Nerissa eats a lot of salads, but unlike a lot of women, she never bothers with pretending like she enjoys them. She munched it with disinterested tolerance, dipping the tines of her fork into the little cup of raspberry vinaigrette and stabbing the little shreds of assorted greens with barely contained disgust. I didn't blame her one bit. I'm even more surly when I have salad. Esme's face was much more neutral as she ate.

"So, what are we going to do?" Esme asked.

I checked my watch. It was now one minute to six. I had no clue whether or not the identity thief was a punctual person or not, but I was pretty sure that he—or possibly she—wasn't here yet. The restaurant didn't have too much of a dinner crowd. Only six tables were occupied, and all of them had at least two people there eating. Our suspect would probably be on his—or her—own.

"We're going to keep an eye on that door and see if a lone person enters and starts scanning the room, looking for somebody."

"And then?"

And then I'll scream, "That's the identity thief, Officer! Arrest him!" If the guy runs, we'll know we have our man, I refrained from saying.

Nerissa swallowed some salad with an expression that made it look like she couldn't wait to get it away from her taste buds as soon as possible. "Funderburke, there's something about this whole thing that doesn't sit well with me."

I had the same unsettling feeling, but I was too desperate to catch the ghoster to admit my misgivings. "Why, you wonder, were we asked to meet at this sandwich shop? Based on the note we intercepted by an extraordinary coincidence, as your father so astutely pointed out, it was imperative for the person we're looking for to remain safely hidden in the motel just a block down the street from us."

"Right. Why not arrange the meeting inside the motel room? Why wouldn't the person coming to visit the ghoster simply pick up some food and any other needed supplies, and then have the consultation in private?"

"Maybe the identity thief is getting stir-crazy from being cooped up in a probably uncomfortable motel, and going out for meals is the only thing keeping him from freaking out," Esme offered.

"After all, the ghoster never did get the message warning about not leaving the motel except to check the P.O. Box and the occasional food run. Maybe our guy's been sneaking out, going to movies and whatnot, possibly blowing his cover."

"But why should there be any need for so much secrecy?" I asked, hating the fact that I had these questions. "After all, we don't know who the "K" in the letter is. We don't have a clue what K looks like or K's real name or anything else. As long as he's not wearing a name tag that says "Hi! My name is Bertie Godspeed" or signing Bertie's name to bad checks all over town, why all this secrecy? The police don't know his real identity—as far as we know—so they're not coming after him. The original credit card fraud and everything else took place in Chicago. Why wouldn't a crook just stay there? It's a big city, and it's actually easier to hide on your home turf, especially when it's a huge, heavily populated urban area, than it is to hide in a smaller area where you don't know anybody and the presence of a stranger skulking around might attract the suspicion of local police. It's not like K is going to be staying in his Aunt Phyllis's guest room. Why stay in a cheap motel in Green Bay? If you're going to flee, why not go even further away, to one of the ocean coasts or even Canada? Or why not pick another big city you can disappear in, or a tiny village in the country? Why here? It just doesn't make any sense."

"Do you think it's a trap?" Nerissa wondered.

"Wait, do you think that someone's going burst in here with a gun and start shooting at us?"

Esme looked pretty nervous, so I took the opportunity to reassure her. "This is way too complex a set-up for an attack. Maybe I'm wrong. It's possible I'm overthinking this. And yet, it's also very possible that I'm being played."

"*We're* overthinking this. *We're* being played," Nerissa corrected.

I accepted the rectification with a grin. It's great to have a reliable partner. "At the same time, I think *we're* probably right to ask the questions *we* just did. It's possible we're missing some crucial information, which could potentially answer some of our concerns. I'd like to be optimistic, but I can't shake the feeling that someone out there's a couple of steps ahead of me—*us*. I thought that I was setting a trap for the ghoster when I sent the letter. Now, I'm getting the sense that there may be a trap, but it's meant for us."

"I agree," Nerissa nodded. "This has all been too easy. The letter just happens to fall out of a guy's sleeve in front of us. You get a quick response telling you exactly when and where to be. This isn't an investigation, it's a gift-wrapped solution."

"Well, we haven't caught the guy yet—" My comment was interrupted by the door chimes ringing, and a man in a shabby sweatshirt and jeans stomped into the restaurant. I can best describe the guy by saying it was like he was trying way too hard to look like a ne'er-do-well. He didn't just walk like a normal person. He sauntered, with his body bobbing with what he must have thought was an intimidating manner. His face was scruffy, there were numerous tattoos on his hands and neck, and he gave off the impression of trying his darnedest to be the toughest guy in the room. He would have been pretty unsettling if not for the fact that there was something indescribably ridiculous about him. I've been around dangerous, violent criminals many times before, and there's an innate hardness in their eyes that can't be duplicated unless you've lived a hard and brutal life. This guy didn't have that. I've seen kids acting like him at Cuthbertson, when we go to sports events or conferences or presentations at inner city schools. Some students try to act like they're totally at home in "the hood." They fool nobody. They might as well rent a billboard with four-foot-tall neon letters that spell out "RICH WHITE KIDS."

Nerissa, Esme, and I exchanged glances and watched him march up to the cashier and say in a voice that was far too loud for a criminal supposedly in hiding, "I've got a reservation for two. The name's Bertie Godspeed."

I didn't know what this guy was up to, but he wasn't acting like a man living in fear of getting caught by the authorities. I gave him a visual once-over and saw no obvious signs of weapons. Making up my mind to act, I stood up, walked up right behind him, and said, "Funny. You don't look like a Bertie Godspeed to me."

He jumped several inches up in the air and whirled around. He looked at me for half a second, and then turned to run. I had a significant advantage in size on him, and it was no trouble at all to grab his arm and drag him towards our table.

"Is there a problem here?" the cashier, a young woman of approximately college age, asked.

"Everything's great. Thank you for asking," I replied in my cheeriest voice as I frog-marched the guy away. I realized that a better place for our conversation would be the booth in the far corner, which didn't have any windows near it he could crash through in an attempt to escape. After shoving him along the bench against the wall, I plonked myself next to him to trap him. Nerissa and Esme joined us a moment later, bringing their salads and drinks along. Nerissa made a second trip and returned with my soup and water.

Suddenly I found myself ferociously hungry. "We're going to have a little chat, 'Bertie,' but first, I'm going to order myself a sandwich. Would you like something? It may be the last nice restaurant meal you have before a long diet of prison food, so I suggest that you choose carefully."

Chapter Eight

I Don't Believe You

Revulsion. That's the best way to describe my feelings as I looked at the fake Bertie Godspeed. Just glancing at this guy made me feel ill. I've said it before, I oppose violence on principle, but I kept becoming aware of my fist clenching under the table, and it took all of my strength to flatten my hand. This fellow was lucky we were in a public place. Not only that, but I noticed that the handful of people who were dining in the restaurant were all looking at us. I suddenly realized that they'd immediately tagged the ghoster as a shady character, and they might have been wondering if Nerissa, Esme, and I were also criminals.

I felt a sudden twist in my duodenum as a worry floated through my mind. I hoped that no one in the restaurant would feel the need to call the police.

My concerns were justified when our waitress came up to our table, and nervously asked, "Is everything all right here?"

With my tongue briefly tied by the realization that there were a dozen pairs of eyes focused on us, it was Nerissa who replied in a voice that made all the silverware on the table vibrate. "Everything's fine. My private investigator boyfriend has just apprehended an identity thief. Thank you for checking. Also, we'd like to order some more food, please."

The waitress blinked five times in rapid succession, and then pulled out her notepad and a pen. Nothing remained of Nerissa's unsatisfying salad but a few smears of vinaigrette, and I knew that wasn't enough for her.

Nerissa ordered a mini-croissant chicken salad sandwich, and Esme asked for a slice of lemon pie. I'd enjoyed the soup, and was about to consider requesting another bowl, when it struck me that it wasn't the best idea to put a substantial quantity of hot liquid within easy reach of a potentially dangerous criminal, so I asked for a tuna melt on rye with provolone with sides of cottage cheese and fruit salad instead. The fourth member of our table wasn't saying anything, so as far as I was concerned, he could starve.

As soon as the waitress left, I leaned over to the ghoster, who was pressing his face against the wall, and said, "Do you want me to call you "Bertie?"

He turned to me, trying to project defiance. "Why not? It's my name."

"Then you won't mind if I take a look at your wallet to check your I.D., will you?"

Immediately, his spine destabilized, and he sagged back against the wall. "I…don't have my wallet on me."

"Did you leave it in your motel room down the block? We can go there with you and look at it."

His eyes widened. "How did you know I'm staying at that motel?"

"I know a lot about you, K." He jumped as I used his initial. "G. hasn't been as careful as you thought."

"Is Grandma going to be in trouble?" His lip quivered, and I decided to take a calculated risk.

"Your Grandma's in a bad situation, K. I don't want to see an old lady go to jail, but…." I let my voice trail off and tried to keep his gaze transfixed on mine. Nerissa can keep a poker face, but Esme was new to this game. I didn't want this guy looking over at her and picking up some cue from her expression that I was bluffing a bit.

I waited patiently as he seemed to make up his mind. Finally, he said, "Look, you've got to let me go. I'm not a bad guy."

I tried not to sneer too much. "Yeah, right. You're a Boy Scout. You just earned your merit badge in identity theft."

"I don't have a clue what you're talking about."

I glared at him so hard it nearly left a bruise. "I don't believe you, you lying handkerchief covered with mucus."

He started hyperventilating. "Look, what if I tell you everything? I won't leave anything out, but if you hear why I did what I did, you'll understand. How's that? Will you let me go then?"

Nerissa and I held each other's gaze for a long time. We can't use mental telepathy, but I figured I knew what she was thinking. "I can't make promises, but I'm a reasonable man. Go on. Make me care about you. Try to convince me to let you go."

I was sure he'd need a lot more prompting, but he started spilling his guts immediately. "Here's what happened. I admit, I haven't always been on the right side of the law."

There's a big surprise, I forced myself to refrain from saying.

"I'm from Chicago. I've stolen a few things in my time, and I've sold a few drugs. I don't have much, man. I'm just doing what I have to in order to survive. You don't get to judge me on that. And you know, I'm not sorry. I do what I gotta do. But I've never hurt anybody, man. I'm not a monster. I'm not violent. If there's trouble, I don't fight, I run. A couple of weeks ago, I was picking up some product, and I saw a guy there shoot another guy. We knew each other, I could identify him, so he fired at me, but he missed, and I got away. I figured he could figure out where I lived, so I hid in a friend's basement for a while, and I called my Grandma to tell her I needed help. Grandma lives in Milwaukee, she's always been good to me. She told me this could be the chance she's been praying for to get me back on the straight and narrow. She said she'd work on getting me a new identity, and she'd give me the chance to get away from Chicago and get a fresh start. A couple days later, she had some documents for me with the name "Bertie Godspeed." Weird name, I thought, but I was desperate. I was willing to take anything. So I used my new identity, came up north, and I've been hiding out here ever since."

We were all quiet for a little bit. I don't claim to be a human lie detector or to have a preternatural ability to see into other people's souls, but I have pretty good instincts, and this guy was metaphorically giving off the stench of the sewer. He didn't look guilty or display any relief after supposedly unburdening his soul. Instead, he looked exhilarated, and there was a glint in his eye that made me suspect he was enjoying himself.

I decided to dig a little deeper. "I know the general details, but not the complete story about how your grandmother got the real Bertie's personal information."

Fake Bertie shrugged. "All I know is that Grandma was at a meeting for that charity, and she found Bertie's birth certificate and other information there and took a few photos with her phone, and that's how she got what she needed."

"Has she ever done anything like this before?"

"Of course not!" Fake Bertie looked indignant. "She's not a criminal."

Yes, she is. If she stole that information, she's a crook, I kept myself from saying. "You have a really caring Grandma. Going out, tracking down the identity of a deceased person for you to use."

"She's the best."

"How did she know how to take those steps, anyway? You said she's never stolen someone's identity before. Did she perform an internet search for "How to ghost somebody?"

He blinked. I could see he was thinking hard. "You know that seniors are at risk for identity theft. Grandma went to a meeting at the library on how to prevent that, and she learned about it there."

His voice was slipping. I don't have a Henry-Higginsesque ear for accents, but I could tell he was trying for a Chicago-area patois… though not from one of the wealthy suburbs. I had no idea what his natural voice was, but his last bit of dialogue sounded distinctly different from how he'd been speaking two minutes ago.

"So your Grandma… what's her first name again?"

I hadn't wanted to telegraph that I didn't know who his grandmother was, but I was hoping he wasn't sharp enough to avoid sharing that information. Instead, I saw a glint in his eye that looked remarkably like intelligence. "You don't know who my grandmother is, do you? You know it was one of those old ladies at the meeting, but you aren't sure which one. Well, I'm not going to tell you."

"You know that the police will figure out who she is quickly enough once we turn you in."

"But you won't do that. You know that if I get put in jail, the guy who I saw commit murder will have me killed in prison, and you don't want that on your conscience. Besides, I could always make some… allegations… that could reflect very negatively on you. I just might be able to get your license revoked if they half believe me. That wouldn't be very pleasant for you, would it? And the authorities might be disposed to be harsh with you, what with your interfering in an open investigation."

Attempting to keep my voice calm and even, I replied. "They might be inimical towards me."

"They certainly would. They'd throw the book at you for digging around on your own. Look, I get it. You're upset that I borrowed your old buddy's name. I understand why you'd be upset. But it's not going to do you any good to hold a grudge. It could wreck your career, and you might even have my blood on your hands. I know I'm not much, but I'm still a human being. So please, just get up, let me go, and head back to Milwaukee."

I grit my teeth. "Look, forget the identity theft for now. What about the murder you witnessed? Why don't you tell the authorities what you saw, get a killer off the streets, and go into the Witness Protection Program? If you have to use a false identity, you might as well get one legitimately."

"I don't trust law enforcement. One of them makes a little slip-up, and I'm dead!"

"The guy whose murder you witnessed is also dead."

Fake Bertie exploded. "Damn it, you act as if you're in kindergarten! This is the big bad world, full of mean people, where nasty things happen!"

A little bell rang in my cranium. "Repeat what you just said, please."

"What?" Fake Bertie suddenly looked scared, as if he knew he'd slipped.

"Forget it." I reached into my coat pocket, and he flinched, as if he was afraid I was going to pull out a knife or a pair of brass knuckles. Instead, my hand gripped my smartphone, and I started performing a quick search.

"What are you doing?" Fake Bertie asked.

"I'm looking up the line you just said. It's very familiar to me." A moment later, I had my answer. "That's a quote from *Wait Until Dark*, a play about a blind woman who has to outwit a trio of criminals who are after a valuable object in her possession. It was made into a movie starring Audrey Hepburn."

Nerissa rooted through her purse and pulled out a packet of moist towelettes. "I think we're on the same page here, Funderburke. I just want to confirm a suspicion. Grab his arm." I complied, and Fake Bertie yelped in dismay as Nerissa seized hold of his hand and started scrubbing away at the tattoo on it. After a little while, it started smearing. She dangled the makeup-stained wipe in front of Fake Bertie's face. "You're an actor, aren't you?"

"You made so many mistakes," I informed him, trying to break his spirit. "Your accent slipped. You said that I was "upset that you borrowed my old buddy's name." How did you know Bertie and I were friends when we were kids? I never said that he was a personal pal. I could've just been hired by somebody to look into this case. When I used the word "inimical," given the context and my expression, you couldn't have known for sure that meant "hostile." It could have meant "sympathetic" or something like that. You knew an SAT-level vocabulary word. I bet you're college-educated. And the line from *Wait Until Dark*. I didn't know Chicago drug dealers were such big Audrey Hepburn fans. In fact..."

I started tapping at my phone again, following my hunch. It took a couple of minutes, but the other three people at the table were staring at me with rapt interest. Finally, the combination of the phrases "Wait Until Dark," "play" and "Chicago" brought me to the webpage of a dinner theater in Inverness. "November 1st to December 20th of last year. The Dine-and-Drama in Inverness presents Frederick Knott's play *Wait Until Dark*." I found one of the cast photos and showed it to Nerissa and Esme. "Featuring Marcus Wahler as Mike Talman." Fake Bertie, who I will now refer to by his real name, sagged. "I don't think you're going to win any Tonys for this performance, Markie."

Five minutes ago, this guy was a swaggering scalawag. Instantaneously, I saw Marcus transform. We were about the same age, but now he looked like a little boy who was dressed as a petty criminal for Halloween, and someone had stolen his bag of candy. His confidence was totally gone, and his defiance had evaporated. He fidgeted, twisting one newly de-tattooed hand inside the other, which was still covered in makeup. "What's going to happen to me?" he finally whimpered.

I started laughing. I couldn't control it. The change was so dramatic, so complete, that it was comical. It was possible that this new persona was a performance as well, but I really doubted his acting skills were up to the task, and this thought made the situation even funnier to me. Nerissa joined in, too, and Esme, who had been trying to keep her expression neutral for the last several minutes, eventually decided it was okay to share in the laughter. Marcus didn't express any merriment, but I caught a flash of hope in his face that indicated that he thought there was a good chance that he wouldn't be spending the night in a prison cell.

When I regained my composure, I turned to him and asked, "So, how did you land this role? Was there a casting call? Did your agent hear about it and get you an audition?"

"Someone telephoned me and asked me to show up at an office in downtown Chicago to try out for a role. When I got there, a really dignified-looking man with gray hair said that he'd seen me in a play recently, and asked if I'd like to stretch my range a little bit. He said he was part of a company that was working on a new interactive mystery game. It was designed for people to play during their free time after work or on weekends. He offered me two hundred dollars a day, set me up in that motel, and told me to check a P.O. Box a couple of times a day. He told me that the plotline was connected to an identity theft story, but he couldn't give me too many more details because every player's game was different. He gave me a script and some basic facts about my character and told me to memorize them. He said I should stick to the basic template provided, but I should feel free to improvise as needed, as long as I didn't go too far afield and add anything that might be a red herring for the players. He also said to underplay, and to resist any urge to ham it up. They told me that the identity theft victim was an old friend of yours, and that you were trying to find out who was behind it. That's all. I thought this was just an interactive game. I swear it."

Nerissa shook her head. "You must have suspected that this was more than just a game. The level of detail, staying at the motel, checking a P.O. Box instead of getting a text or an email like normal people communicate… You knew something was off, didn't you?"

He squirmed. "All right, I figured that there was something shady here, but nothing serious like a murder. I figured there must be some sort of con or something like that going on, but do you know how hard it is to make a living as a stage actor in the Midwest? I figured whatever was happening, I wasn't going to hurt anybody, and I'd have plausible deniability if the police got involved. And yes, I thought it would be fun to play a character like this."

I completely believed him. Of course, he was raising more questions than he was answering. "What was the gray-haired guy's name?"

"Mr. Jones."

I was fairly certain this was a pseudonym. "Did he tell you to dress like this and apply the temporary tattoos?"

"No, that was all my idea. I thought that it might give my performance a little added authenticity."

"It certainly added *something*, I'll give you that. So, you got my letter?"

"Yes. I called Mr. Jones, sent him a picture of the letter, and he called me back, telling me to text you, set up everything, and to get you to meet me here at six."

"Did he tell you who to expect?"

"He didn't give me your name. He just said to walk in and announce to the cashier that I was "Bertie Godspeed" in a loud voice, and to expect a tall, dark man in a long black leather coat to come up to me and ask me questions. He also said it was likely that a brunette with lengthy hair and shiny clothes would be there, too," Marcus added with a nod towards Nerissa. He turned to Esme. "He didn't say anything about you, but I just went with it."

I interrogated him a little while longer, asking questions he couldn't answer, at least not fully. The waitress arrived with our food, and now that I was feeling a lot warmer towards Marcus, I suggested that he order something for himself, and soon the waitress brought him an iced tea and chicken salad on a bed of lettuce. Now that I figured he wouldn't throw it at me, I ordered myself some more soup, too. The conversation shifted in tone from hostile interrogation to friendly getting to know each other. In his real personality, Marcus seemed like a pretty decent guy, and he was appalled to hear the true details of Bertie's story.

"What do you want me to do now?" he asked.

I looked at Nerissa. "I think it might be a good idea to allow Mr. Jones and whoever he's working with believe that we've been fooled, at least for a little while longer."

She nodded. "I agree. Marcus, you should tell him that we bought everything you were saying. Maybe explain that you started crying, telling us how you feared for your life, the man in the leather coat was so angry. Don't mention the fake tattoos and wardrobe choice. Just tell them we accepted your story of witnessing a murder, and your awesome grandma found you an identity to use."

"Absolutely. Also, say that when I left, I told you, 'You're using the name of a great human being. Make sure you live up to it.'"

Marcus beamed. "That's a great line. Love it. I gotta write it down." He borrowed a pen from me and started scribbling on the back of the paper placemat.

We brainstormed a little bit more, making sure there were no obvious problems with the plan, and by eight we realized we had to head home, as we had to drive all the way back to Milwaukee and be up in the morning for work. Each of us shook hands with Marcus, and I drove him back to his motel—an establishment so disreputable-looking that if I had to pick a place to stay on a road trip, given the choice, I would unhesitatingly prefer to stay at an establishment owned by Norman Bates.

In the years that followed, Marcus would become a regular performer at the Milwaukee Rep. Nerissa, and I have never missed a production in which he's appeared. He's really talented when he has a well-written and plotted script memorized, and he's gotten better every season. Improv isn't his strongest suit. That and dancing are his weak points. But give him some decent dialogue and a character he can work with, and he's a delight. Left to his own devices, he tends to overplay a role, but under the guidance of a skilled director, he's a superb actor.

During the first half-hour of our ride back to Milwaukee, Esme and I said nothing, as Nerissa had received a frantic message from one of her girls, who was locked in her bedroom with her fourteen-month-old son after her mother and a man her mother had met two hours earlier in a bar had consumed some sort of hallucinogenic drug and were now screaming and throwing every item in the apartment lighter than their own body weights at each other. The suggestion that it might be sensible to call the police was immediately rejected, as the girl in question refused to let her mother be arrested and probably sent to prison. Nerissa solved the problem by calling a few friends of mine who work for a private security firm that pays light years better than my first P.I. job, and sending them to rescue the girl and her baby, while getting the two so-called adults medical attention. She called the others on my phone, as her student begged Nerissa not to hang up on her. Esme and I were caught in the position of trying not to eavesdrop while being incapable of ignoring the unfolding drama, as the screaming and thudding in the background steadily reached unsettling levels. As it turned out, the mother and the not-so-gentlemanly caller were unable to escape the police after all, as the inhabitants of the neighboring apartments had no compunction about calling 911. By the time my friends arrived, the police had dragged the pair away, but Nerissa's student and her baby were left safely in the closet. They managed to calm her down, help her pack up her things, and take the pair of them to her aunt's house on the south side of town. Nerissa promised to have breakfast with her at Cuthbertson first thing in the morning to discuss matters, and by the time she was finally able to end the call, she was sagging from emotional exhaustion.

None of us said anything for a long time. We were just going through Manitowoc when Esme finally asked, "I'm sorry. I don't know if this is the right time, but you made it sound like you know who stole Bertie's identity. Who was it?"

"Well, think about it," I replied. "The whole case hinges on who had the opportunity to get the information that allowed the ghoster to apply for credit cards and loans and whatnot under Bertie's name. It's not like in the past, when people would walk through graveyards and find names and birth dates of people, often children who died young. They needed his Social Security number and other details. It's unlikely the ghoster had access to government records. Therefore, it seems likely that the information was taken from the Godspeeds' personal files. Who had access to that? The Godspeeds themselves, but I'm sure you'll agree, knowing what we do about them, that Mr. and Mrs. Godspeed would never do anything like that, and that young Zita's an unlikely suspect as well. Among a dozen objections to her potential guilt is the fact that she couldn't possibly have gone to Chicago to make the credit card purchases—at least, not without her extended absence being detected by her family or friends."

"Absolutely right," Esme nodded.

"So, who else is there to consider? Who else makes frequent visits to the Godspeed home? They don't have a cleaning person. They don't have too much extended family. Mr. Godspeed's sister Yolanda would no more exploit Bertie's identity than he would. Now, Nerissa and I go to their house for dinner all the time...."

"But we know we didn't do it," Nerissa added.

"We did not. Who does that leave? There is one other person with frequent access to the Godspeeds' home, and by extension, Bertie's old personal documents. Someone who the Godspeeds trust completely. That person has worked with them at Bertie's Buddies for many years. The individual in question has had countless opportunities to check their old files. I don't know very much about this person's financial situation, but I know she hasn't made a dime from all of her countless hours volunteering for the Godspeeds."

"It wasn't me." There was no indignation or anger in Esme's voice. I think she knew I didn't really suspect her.

"Well, I don't have any hard evidence exonerating you, but let's assume that I accept your story. So who did do it? Who had the opportunity? It's definitely possible there was an opening that I don't know about, but right now, the only chance that someone I haven't mentioned yet had to gain this information is at that recent board of directors meeting at the Godspeeds' house. The documents—Bertie's birth certificate, his Social Security card, whatever else—were there."

"You know the four other people at that meeting," Nerissa chimed in. "Of those four, which of them would be the one you suspect the most?"

Esme didn't say her name, but she shifted in her seat. "I don't want to say her name without proof."

"It's just us here," I assured her. "No risk of a slander lawsuit. But even though I was pretty sure it was her ever since this afternoon, it was what Marcus said that convinced me. It was that story he was fed about the world's best grandmother getting the information for him. When I sent that letter to the P.O. Box, I thought that I was setting the trap, when in fact, the person behind the theft was trying to trap me. Not a very elegant one. The goal was to persuade me that Marcus's grandmother was the culprit, even though I wouldn't be told which elderly lady it was. But that wasn't the point. If I was gullible enough to believe that the identity thief was a grandmother, then I'd believe that one of the three grandmothers at the meeting was guilty. And with the three grandmas in the crosshairs, the fourth person at—"

My phone rang. I never answer my phone when I'm driving, but Nerissa knows the drill. She reached into my coat pocket and gasped a bit as she read the caller ID. "It's Vianne Coquina. Shall I put her on speakerphone?"

I did a bit of quick mental calculating. "Yes, please." As soon as Nerissa tapped the button and held it up for me, I said, "Hello, Vianne. We were just talking about you."

"I imagine you were," her voice replied. "I'd like to talk to you. I suppose you're still about an hour away from Milwaukee right now?"

"About that, yes."

"Would you mind meeting me to talk tonight?"

"It's getting late, and it's a school night—"

"You know you want to hear what I have to say. Where would you like to meet?"

Nerissa whispered, "Cuthbertson," and I agreed with her plan. "I'll be at Cuthbertson Hall in an hour, give or take a few minutes. If you want to talk to me tonight, go to the entrance to the Upper School. The security guard on duty should still have your driver's license on file from your visit today. Tell him you're there to speak to me, assuming I don't get there first."

"Deal. See you then."

I zoomed off into the night, anticipating a showdown. I know for a fact that Nerissa and Esme said a lot of things over the next fifty-five minutes, but I can't recall a single one of them. All I know is that it was just after ten o'clock when I pulled into the Cuthbertson Upper School parking lot, and Vianne was already there, standing at the entryway and speaking into the intercom. She appeared to be having some trouble convincing the guard to let her in, but as soon as the guard saw me, he buzzed us all inside.

"Would you care to come into my office?" I asked her.

"No, I've heard the stories about how you have it wired for sound and video. What about the library reading room?"

That was as good a place as any, so the four of us made our way there, and settled in four comfy chairs around a small round table in the corner. "All right. What do you want to tell me?" I asked.

"First, take out your phones so I can confirm you're not recording this." We all complied with Vianne's request, though I insisted that she do the same, just so we were all on the same footing. She complied without comment.

"Of course, you could have some other device in one of your coat pockets."

"I could, but I do not have one, and I am not recording you, and if you insist on searching me, I'm going to walk out and go home right now, Vianne."

She looked at Nerissa and Esme. "Do they both have to be here?"

"Yes."

"You don't want to be alone with me?"

"No."

"Are you afraid for your own safety, or are you worried about what you might do to me if they're not here to stop you?"

"Either get to the point or go home, Vianne."

Vianne's lips and eyes twitched for a few seconds, and then sighed. "Fair enough. There's no point in stretching this out, especially as it's all gone downhill. It's late, and I won't waste time. Marcus called me shortly after speaking with you. He told me exactly what you wanted him to say."

I made no reply, not wanting to give away anything. Nerissa kept a poker face as well, but Esme didn't have the practice we did. If Vianne had any doubt that we'd managed to compel Marcus to break character, Esme's expression confirmed that we'd gotten him to crack.

"I could tell at once that he was lying," Vianne continued. "After all of these years with my husband, I've developed a pretty perceptive sense for when a man's not being honest with me." The look she shot me was supposed to be piercing. I tried to indicate through my facial expression that I was completely unaffected by her gaze. She seemed to know exactly what I was trying to convey. "I'm being completely straight with you. I'd appreciate it if you'd demonstrate the same level of respect to me."

Leaning forward slightly, I asked her, "Given what you did, and how you know I feel about my friend's identity being stolen, and how it's affected the Godspeeds, who have never gotten any kind of closure over their son's murder, I think you can understand why I'm not impressed with the level of respect that you've shown other people lately."

The color rose in Vianne's face, and she opened her mouth only to shut it again before she could produce a sound. After a few moments of consideration, she nodded and answered. "That's fair."

"Is that an admission of guilt?"

I could practically see the words "the hell with it" flashing through Vianne's eyes as she made up her mind. "Yes. I admit it. When I went to the Godspeeds' house for the meeting recently, I saw Bertie's information and realized it was a golden opportunity for me. I had a minute by myself with the papers, and I photographed all of them on my phone."

The flaming anger shooting through my body must have been obvious to my three companions. I think I would have burst into a tirade at the top of my lungs if I hadn't felt Nerissa's incredibly soft hand on mine. It had a remarkably soothing effect on my disposition. I let her run her fingers up and down over my knuckles, and before very long I regained my composure. It took a bit of effort, but I was able to speak in a civil tone at a modest decibel level.

"Let me ask you something, Vianne. Your clothes are expensive. I assume your jewelry's real. The care and maintenance for your hairstyle isn't cheap, either. Maybe there's something going on with your financial situation I'm not aware of, but why exactly did you feel the need to ghost Bertie all for the sake of, at most, a few thousand dollars?"

Vianne's face was expressionless as she answered my question. "I don't need the money. I did it for my brother."

"What's his name?"

"Garrett Andexler." Nerissa and I exchanged glances. We'd heard that last name in the news from time to time. The Andexler family were reasonably prominent in the Chicago social scene, ran a few highly successful businesses, and every so often, there was a blurb in the newspapers about how they had donated a massive chunk of money to fund a hospital or something similarly worthy. All over the Midwest, there were school auditoriums and cancer wards and atriums in local buildings with their name on them."

"I'm surprised that you don't use your maiden name more often," I replied. "With all of the charity work and outreach you do, going by Vianne Andexler Coquina might be a useful asset."

"Most of my family and I are not on good terms," Vianne sighed. *Join the club*, I thought to myself right before she continued, saying, "I severed ties with the majority of my relatives several years ago when I found out how they make the majority of their money. I'm not going to go into any details on that topic. I promised that I'd tell you everything about my role in the identity theft, but this matter is private."

I was intrigued by the Andexler family's dirty laundry, but I knew to keep my eyes on the prize. "Fair enough."

"Part of the story I gave to "Mr. Jones"—a longtime ally, by the way, you don't need to know anything else about him—coached Marcus to tell you was inspired by true events. Garrett is my baby brother. We've always been close, and I look out for him. He developed a drug habit in high school, and ever since, he's been in trouble with the law."

"And he actually witnessed a murder, like in Marcus' story?"

"No. I made the story a bit worse than it really was. I thought it would make the narrative more compelling, but I now realize it was overkill."

"Yes, it was."

"What really happened is that Garrett was robbing a house—my parents cut him off a while back, so he's desperate for cash to fuel his habit. He had a couple of friends, also addicts, with him. The owner of the house caught them, and one of Garrett's pals with him punched the guy out, and they all escaped. This is the first time Garrett's ever been involved in something violent, and he was afraid his friend had seriously hurt the guy. It was a life-changing moment for him."

"Was the victim seriously injured?"

"Thank God, no. The blow left him unconscious, and he knocked out one of the guy's teeth, but the poor man will be fine. Garrett didn't know it at the time, though. It took a while, and I had to pull a few favors but I managed to find out exactly what happened. Luckily, my father made some contributions to the hospital where the victim was treated."

"I thought you said you severed ties with most of your family."

"Just because I don't talk to them, it doesn't mean that I have any scruples about using the Andexler name when it suits my purposes." She paused. "I'm not trying to justify my actions."

"That's good, because you're not succeeding."

"That was harsh."

"That was accurate." I knew I should have been diplomatic, but it was late, I had been driving for well over four hours, and I was in no mood for niceties.

Additionally, I wasn't completely convinced by Vianne's confession. When you're trying to evaluate if someone's telling you the truth or not, you have to go by a combination of logic and instinct, and right now, my gut and my brain were telling me that Vianne wasn't making this story up out of whole cloth. I got the sense she was telling me the truth... just not the whole truth. Maybe she was polishing something up here and there. A little bowdlerization and a trace of obfuscation can clean up a story nicely.

I wasn't even sure that she was the one editing the narrative. As a naturally suspicious man, I wouldn't be surprised if Garrett was the one who'd thrown the punch, and indeed, that he had no partners at all in the robbery. Perhaps he'd told his sister a version of the story that was carefully tailored to make himself look better.

"I'm telling you the truth here." That was a mistake on Vianne's part.

Whenever someone indignantly declares that they're being totally honest, my nostrils detect the effluvia of male bovine excrement. "My brother called me, asking him to help him, because he was worried that his partners in crime were going to come after him to make sure he didn't tell the police what they done. He was in fear for his life, and he didn't know what else to do. He needed to get away and hide, and to do that, he needed a fresh identity. He didn't know where to find one, and neither did I, so I grabbed the first one I could find. I was looking out for his safety. Surely you understand."

"Why couldn't you just invite him up to Milwaukee and have him stay in your basement?" Nerissa asked.

It was a reasonable question, but from the look on Vianne's face, you would have thought that Nerissa had suggested that Vianne ought to have sprouted wings and flown to the moon. "My husband doesn't get along with Garrett, and he's tapped out most of my money…what are you doing? Put that down!"

Nerissa had picked up her phone and was tapping rapidly. "Relax. I'm not recording anything, but if you're not comfortable, just be quiet."

I spoke over Vianne's indignant gasp. "There's more to it than what you've told us, isn't there?"

"I've told you everything you needed to know."

"Not about why you decided to pull that stunt. You paid a homeless drug addict to drop that envelope in front of me. You hired an actor to pretend to be an identity thief. Why bother? Why not leave it alone?"

"I know your reputation, Funderburke. I knew this would be personal for you, and I knew you wouldn't let it go. I thought you'd keep obsessing about it until you found out who stole your friend's identity, and I thought if I made you work for it, you'd be more willing to believe the story and leave it alone." Either Vianne believed that Nerissa wasn't recording her, or she was too upset to worry about it.

"Who is Mr. Jones?"

"A very capable man who makes his living acting as a go-between for people who need help with tricky situations. I don't know his real name, but my husband has him on retainer. I figured I could trust Mr. Jones to be discreet with this."

"Okay…. When did you find out I knew about the case? I only saw you a little while before the whole Dallan-and-the-envelope thing happened. That wasn't enough time to devise your plan."

"I spoke to her on the phone not long after you called Mrs. Godspeed after you found out about Bertie being ghosted," Esme explained. "I mentioned you, and I told her I wouldn't be surprised if you started to look into it."

After a few seconds of mulling over that point, I had another question. "All right. Then what about the police? Why weren't you as concerned about them as you were about me?"

"Put the phone down, please, Nerissa," Vianne asked.

"I'll go into the next room. Be back in a minute."

As soon as Nerissa left the room, Vianne explained, "I did a little reconnaissance on the two detectives handling the case. They have remarkably low clearance rates, and they're both set to retire in the next couple of months. I figured I shouldn't lose too much sleep over their solving the mystery. You, on the other hand, were a different matter. I know how you brought down that law firm you used to work for because you wouldn't let go of your personal crusade."

"All right. Let's say I buy all of that. I know I saw through the whole thing with Marcus, but you didn't know for a fact that I'd deduced that you were behind it all. Why are you telling me all of this now?"

"Because I want you to hear my side of the story before it all comes out. After giving him his new identity, I told my brother to get a passport and a car and go over the border to Canada. Instead, he stayed in Chicago and continued to get high. He did buy a car, but he crashed it into a fast food restaurant a few hours ago. He called me to tell me what happened, and told me he couldn't get away because his legs were broken. When the ambulance arrived, he told me not to worry and hung up. Ha! He forgot that still has the credit cards and everything else with "Bertie Godspeed" on them. I thought when the police came to investigate, they'd find everything, and Garrett would spill his guts… So I wanted to speak to you first. Consider it a professional courtesy."

More likely, you wanted to run your story by me first before you told it to the police and see if I caught any holes you could patch up, I thought to myself. Before I could reply, Vianne's phone rang. She glanced at me, I gestured to show I had no problem with her answering, and she grabbed her phone and held it to her ear.

As soon as I saw her expression changing, I knew the news was terrible. After a couple of minutes, she lowered her phone into her lap, and tears started welling up in her eyes.

"What's wrong?"

"That was the hospital. Apparently, my brother's injuries were worse than he thought. He passed away ten minutes ago."

Chapter Nine

What Really Happened

We all sat quietly for a few moments, and then I saw the tears running down Vianne's face. For the first time that night, I was certain she was displaying a genuine emotional reaction, devoid of guile or exaggeration. I handed her a tissue from my coat pocket, and she accepted it without thanking me. She dabbed her eyes, blew her nose, and then without a word, she leapt to her feet and sprinted out the door, past Nerissa, and down the corridor.

Nerissa re-entered the reading room. "What happened?"

I brought her up to speed, and Nerissa flopped back into the chair next to me. "Wow."

Esme rose to her feet. "I have a six-thirty meeting in the morning. I should probably get going." We started to say our goodbyes, but Esme's face changed. "Thank you for letting me come with you tonight. It's hard to explain, but it was really important to me that you let me see what happened. The Godspeeds...I think I said this already, but they've been the parents I always wished I had. This whole situation has hurt them in ways I can't bear to see, and I wanted to play a part in catching the guy behind it."

"It didn't turn out the way any of us expected," Nerissa shrugged.

"No... What's going to happen to her?"

"This could go down a lot of different ways. We'll just have to see," I sighed. "My gut tells me that she's not going to face any jail time."

"Why not?"

I was about to answer, but I caught myself before going on a tangent. "It'll take a long time for me to explain all my thoughts. Are you sure you want to wait to hear all I have to say?"

Esme blushed. "I don't want to give offense, but like I said, I need to get home and grab some sleep."

When it was just me and Nerissa in the reading room, she arched an eyebrow and said, "Two hours. Tops."

"Two hours for what?"

"That's how much sleep you're going to get tonight. You're going to obsess about this way past midnight, and then you're going to realize it's nearly three-thirty in the morning, and you'll force yourself to go to bed, but you're not going to be able to sleep, and you'll stare at the ceiling until well after five, until your adrenaline finally runs out and you pass out, only to wake up less than a hundred and twenty minutes later when your alarm goes off. Then you're going to be a slug all day tomorrow, and the next couple of days, too, unless somehow you manage to hit the sack early enough tomorrow night to get twelve full hours, which I doubt."

"You know me so well. Even if you've never actually been there to watch me sleep through the night, you've heard me complain when I've gotten crummy rest often enough. So, what did you find out from your Internet search?"

"I found a few profiles on the Andexler family here. Some of them dated back over a decade ago. There's no mention of Vianne anywhere."

"Think she made up the family connection?"

"Maybe. But look at this photo of Mr. and Mrs. Andexler and their three known children." She handed me her phone.

"What about it?"

"Look at the patriarch of the family. He and Vianne have the same eyes. But I don't see any resemblance to Ma Andexler."

"Are you suggesting…"

"I'm not going to say my theory out loud. I just wonder what sort of family man Mr. Andexler really is."

Nerissa soon made it clear she needed to get back home so she could get as much rest as possible. I told her to go on home, and that I was just going to sit here for a while and think. Nerissa was having none of it. She informed me that if she left me here, I'd just sit here and stew until dawn. After an indignant denial that neither of us believed, she tugged at my arm for a while until I finally got up and walked back down to the parking lot with her.

She was totally right about my sleep that night. I only managed somewhere between half an hour and forty-five minutes of rest. I remember very little of the next day. Fortunately, there was no call for me to substitute teach on Wednesday, and as my duties were light and spread out, I was able to snatch three substantial naps in the privacy of my office, and that evening I collapsed on my bed without any dinner and seized fourteen uninterrupted hours of blissful slumber.

Thursday and Friday passed with sporadic bits of interest regarding Bertie's ghosting. When the late Garrett's clothes had been examined, they had found various items of identification sporting his real name, and several others bearing Bertie's. The police officers assigned to investigate the identity theft were called in, but despite my best efforts, I received no inside information as to their inquiries. I did learn that the police had questioned Vianne, but as far as I could tell, the interview was a short one.

Once I'd gotten my head on straight, I'd called the Godspeeds and set up a meeting right after school ended on Wednesday. I gave them a full account of my adventures in Green Bay, what I'd learned, and what I'd deduced. Mr. Godspeed excused himself and left my office, saying that he needed to take a walk to clear his head and that he'd be back soon. Zita was furious, and she started vowing vengeance on Vianne, only to be soothed by her more tranquil mother.

"How can you say that! Why don't you want her in jail?" Zita asked her mother.

"Let me tell you something," Mrs. Godspeed sighed. "Your father and I had a very difficult road to being parents. We tried for five years before we had Bertie, and by that point the doctors told us we would probably never be able to conceive. Not for any discernable reason, it was just one of those things.

And then Bertie came, and he made us happier than we've ever been. We hoped to give him siblings, but none came for thirteen years. You know what happened next. I thought it was the end of the world, and I nearly fell apart. I started collapsing all the time, falling violently ill frequently, until finally, your Aunt Yolanda yelled at your father to snap out of his own depression and take me to the hospital. That's when I found out I'd be having you. I've never brought this up before, but not long ago, I started worrying that you might see yourself as...a replacement for Bertie."

Zita stirred in her chair. "I have wondered...."

"That's not what happened. You were on your way before Bertie died, though we didn't know it at the time. We'd wanted someone like you for most of our lives, but we'd given up hope. And then, just when our world had crumbled around us, and I didn't see the point of going on, we found out there was a reason to keep going. And I'm so glad we did." Mrs. Godspeed rubbed her temples, as she always does when she feels a stress headache on the rise. I brought her a glass of water for her pills, and she thanked me and continued. "My point is, I know how losing someone you love can destroy you. Whatever Vianne's done, she's been punished enough."

Zita did not look convinced. "What do you think, Funderburke?"

"I really do not know. I've met a lot of nasty people in my time, and I've seen a bunch of individuals who have just made some very stupid decisions. And from what I've seen of Vianne, she doesn't seem to fall into either of those categories. She knew what she was doing. And yet... All of my instincts that set off alarm bells when I come into contact with a terrible person are dormant now. I don't think that she's a villain. I want to believe that when she stole Bertie's identity, she did it out of love and desperation for her brother. Basically decent people, or at least people who could be moral individuals if they just listened to their consciences, make mistakes. All the same... the way she was telling that story to me last night, and the unnecessarily complex way she set up that false solution for me... I get the sense that she's an experienced liar, but she's not really comfortable or happy about diverging from the truth."

"So what are you saying?"

"A week ago, I was furious at the unknown person who had ghosted Bertie.

Today, I'm angry at her, but I'm not filled with the violent, seething rage that I feel towards several of the other people in my life who've done me wrong in the past."

Zita sniffed. "Does that mean that you're going to be her pen pal while she's in prison? Are you going to send her cookies to share with her cellmates?"

"I'm not sure that she'll go to jail."

"Why not? She confessed in front of three witnesses."

"Yes, and I'm wondering why the police haven't interviewed me, Nerissa, and Esme yet. When she spoke to us last night, she figured that the police would make her brother crack, and then they'd come after her. Now, without her brother telling his side of the story, it's possible that she could preemptively go to the police with a story that made her look less culpable, or maybe even an innocent victim compelled to do something against her will."

"You really think she'll get away with it?" The horror in Zita's eyes broke my heart.

"I don't know. All I can say is that she strikes me as a survivor. And she's well-connected. She may or may not be linked by blood to a wealthy and powerful family, and her husband... well, you know him." Not for the first time, I wondered why the two of them got together.

We covered a lot of the same ground over and over again, until, finally, the Godspeeds left for home, and I confirmed that I'd help them deliver the meals that weekend.

Flashing forward to Saturday evening, the Meals on Wheels dry run turned out to be a major success, and we were holding a little celebration at one of our favorite Italian restaurants in the Story Hill neighborhood of Milwaukee. Aside from me, Nerissa, and the Godspeeds, Mrs. Zwidecker, and Esme, we were accompanied by a handful of donors and other people connected to Bertie's Buddies who I didn't know.

We were all eating and having a good time when two people I didn't expect would have the guts to show their faces arrived. Tyler and Vianne Coquina walked into our corner of the dining room. Vianne at least had the decency to look uncomfortable, and Tyler had the face of a man who has never known shame and never will.

Tyler immediately started walking around the table, slapping people on the back with hands that I hoped—but doubted—had been well-washed. A line from *My Fair Lady* reverberated through my head, where Professor Henry Higgins sings (or rather, speaks somewhat rhythmically, in Rex Harrison's rendition), "*Oozing* charm from e'vry pore, he *oiled* his way across the floor."

Fortunately, I was against the wall, so Tyler couldn't make his way towards me easily. Vianne was standing in one corner and showing no desire to leave it, so I decided to make the first move. Forcing ersatz friendliness into my voice, I called out to her, "Vianne! Come over here and join us!" I stood up, grabbed a chair from an empty table, set it between mine and Nerissa's and gestured at her to sit in it in a manner that she couldn't gracefully refuse.

Vianne lowered herself into the chair as if I'd wired it with a lethal amount of electricity. She gave my face a thorough examination and eventually decided that I wasn't going to seize my table knife and use it to stab her in the throat. "How are you, Funderburke? Nerissa?"

"I'm concerned about you," I replied. "I know you've gone through a terrible loss, and I never got the chance to give you my proper condolences."

The three of us were a bit apart from the others, and the ambient music playing over the restaurant speakers, coupled with Tyler's attempt to be the center of attention for the other diners, masked our conversation substantially.

"I'm as well as can be expected," she replied.

"How is your father?" Nerissa asked with emphasis on the last word, but no malice.

"I think he's relieved to have one of his little embarrassments out of the picture more than anything else. His wife's probably ecstatic. My half-siblings don't know I exist, as far as I know." Vianne looked at us in turn. "I assume you've done the sort of digging a private eye's trained to do?"

I had, indeed. It was easy, if you know how to do it, to find the records of Vianne's marriage to Tyler, and to discover that her birth first name was Veruca, which I thought was a moniker given only to Roald Dahl characters. Probably at some point, she had stressed her middle name, calling herself V.

Anne on documents, before blending her initial and middle name together. Her maiden name, which was the same as her brother's, was fairly distinctive, and it took no more than four minutes to discover that a woman by that name had once worked for the Andexler patriarch around the time that Vianne and her brother had been born. This woman was now in prison after being convicted of multiple counts of fraud.

At Vianne's urging, I quietly informed her of almost everything I'd found out, withholding a few of the more salacious details out of a mixture of chivalry and squeamishness.

"Then you're aware that the case is closed?"

By using what the Godspeeds had been told by the authorities and a few contacts I won't name, I'd learned that there would be no charges against Vianne. "Apparently, they believe that you were threatened by your brother to find him a new identity to use."

"I understand you were able to convince the powers that be that you were in fear for your life," Nerissa looked at Vianne with an expression that nobody who knew her well could have taken for genuine concern. "It must have been so terrible for you."

"Yes…" Vianne turned towards me. "Would you mind telling me what you're going to do?"

I met her gaze. "I'm going to respect the Godspeeds' wishes. At least Mr. and Mrs. Godspeeds'. Zita wants you to fry."

Vianne looked dumbfounded. "Just what are the Godspeeds' wishes?"

"You don't know? Maybe I should let them tell you."

"No! I want to be told now!" Vianne forgot to keep her voice low, and everybody else looked over at us for a few moments before Tyler regained their unwilling attention.

"After a lot of discussion," I explained, "Mr. and Mrs. Godspeed want you to remain on the Board of Directors for Bertie's Buddies."

"What? Why?"

"You expected them to kick you out and never speak to you again?"

"Well…yeah. Why wouldn't they?"

"A couple of reasons. One of them is *not* the fact that they're concerned about the money they might lose if they don't have access to the funds that your husband might bring in to them."

Vianne actually smiled. "An awful lot of people run non-profits to make a profit. The Godspeeds aren't that sort of people. That's one reason I wanted to work with them in the first place. But why do they still want me to work with them?"

"Part of it is that repeated contact with you might help with the forgiveness process. Also, I think they feel a bit sorry for you. With your mother sporadically... unavailable to parent you, and going in and out of foster homes, they're rather impressed with your resilience and your ability to pull yourself up by your own bootstraps."

"I tried to help Garrett," she sighed. "I got myself scholarships and part-time jobs. He wanted none of it."

"He made his choices."

"Yes, he did. It doesn't make me feel better, though." Vianne paused for a moment before asking, "There's another reason, isn't there?"

"There might be."

"Is it a case of keeping your friends close and your enemies closer? Do they want to keep an eye on me to make sure that I don't get into any more mischief?"

"That's a bit cynical, isn't it?" Nerissa asked, deftly evading the question.

"One thing my life with my mother taught me, if you expect the worst from people, you may not be happy, but you'll be right more often than not."

"Your assessment of the Godspeeds' motives is a bit unfair," I informed her. "They've seen how you've worked with them over the past year, and they think that your heart may not be pure, but you're the sort of person who's worth fighting for. They're concerned for your soul."

"My soul." I couldn't tell if Vianne's laugh was bitter or sad. "I haven't thought about that in a while. I think I had one of those once. I'm pretty sure all those years with my mother killed it."

"The Godspeeds have an admirable habit of not giving up on people," I informed her. "I'm trying to emulate them, but it's not easy."

"No offense," Nerissa said, "but it's best you find something to do with your time other than planning crimes. Hiring that drug addict to drop the envelope? Setting up the whole run-around in Green Bay to provide us with a false reason for the ghosting? Way too complicated."

"I know. Plotting was never my strong point. After one disaster, Mom told me that she'd never work with me on a scheme again unless I—"

Tyler slithered up to us. "It's been lovely stopping by to join in on the celebration, but we have a fundraiser to attend."

"Leaving so soon? This party won't be the same without you," Nerissa said in a voice that only the tone-deaf or extremely vain could have mistaken for being dripping with sweetness.

Chuckling, Tyler said, "I'm sure we'll see each other again soon. Oh, what a lovely blouse you're wearing." Nerissa was sporting her new green satin shirt with the embossed snakeskin pattern. She didn't exactly smack his hand away when he tried to feel it, but she managed to deflect his libidinous pawing in a way that was both polite and firm, while protecting her skin from having to make direct contact with him and not having to grab the cutlery from the table. It was unclear as to whether he got the hint or not, given the way his eyes were running back and forth over her.

As Vianne rose from her chair, and I stood up with her out of habit, Tyler said, "Funderburke, buddy, would you walk us out? I wanted to have a quick word with you." Vianne shot me a look that clearly said, "What the hell is he up to now?" I was asking the same question myself, so I followed them towards the door. Nerissa wasn't specifically invited, and by joining us, she was exposing herself to the very real risk that Tyler would go for a goodbye hug, but curiosity overruled prudence, and she was right behind me on the way to the exit.

As Tyler buttoned up his topcoat, which was probably cashmere, costing more than Nerissa's car, he leaned forward towards me and said, "Funderburke, I really respect the work you do. And I really think that you should focus on helping those kids now. It's in your best interest to leave this matter alone now. If you keep digging around, I'd have to call in a few favors from some powerful friends of mine. And you wouldn't like that, I'm sure."

He shot me the kind of smile that I imagine pythons give rats right before they unhinge their jaws and swallow them whole. There are many ways to deal with a threat like that. I thought rapidly, and quickly decided upon the best response. I threw my head back and laughed as if I'd just heard the funniest thing I'd ever come across in my life. After fifteen seconds of convincing chuckling, I slapped him hard on the shoulder and said, "Good one, Tyler. That's hilarious."

He looked utterly flabbergasted. People who think they're threatening are often gobsmacked when people treat them like a ridiculous joke. He opened his mouth, I forestalled him with another round of guffawing in the general direction of his face, and with a bemused expression, he walked out of the restaurant without a word.

Vianne smiled. "Well done. I wish more people treated him like the buffoon he is."

"Mind if I ask you an impertinent question?" Nerissa asked. "Why did you marry him?"

"I was given my choice of options to get out of a situation, and I picked the one I thought would be the least painful. Live and learn. I should've chosen prison." As she put her hand on the door, Vianne turned back to us and said, "Maybe I'll tell you about that someday. You can believe me or not, but I really do like you both. I hope that maybe we can become genuine friends eventually. It'd mean a lot to me."

We didn't have a reply to that, and Vianne walked out into the night. We would cross paths with the Coquinas many times over the following years, but it would be over three months before we saw them again.

"What are you thinking?" Nerissa asked.

"A few hours ago, I wanted her thrown in a jail cell for a long time. Now, I'm realizing that she's in a marriage that is a lot more excruciating for her than any prison sentence."

"That last comment is sticking with me. I wonder if she has any friends. I kind of doubt that she does."

"Do you want to want to rush out and invite her to an afternoon of shopping and manicures and girl talk?"

"Ha-ha. Actually, I just might do something like that someday. I really want to know what's going on in her head."

Our discussion about Vianne was interrupted by Esme. "Well? What did she have to say?"

I gave Esme a quick summary of events, and she gave a low whistle. "Wow. So that's it, then? You're just going to leave her to her own rotten life?"

"That's the plan for now," I informed her, "but I reserve the right to change my mind at any time."

"Well, if the Godspeeds are okay with the situation, then I guess I am, too. How long have we been here? What time is it?"

I glanced at my wristwatch and held the dial out to her as I answered. "Eight-thirty-two. We've been here a couple of hours."

Esme nodded. "I'm a short-hitter these days. I think we should order dessert, and then I need to get home and turn in. That's a really nice watch, by the way. That just goes to show how much the Godspeeds value your presence in their lives and your friendship with Bertie, by giving you that." Esme started walking back to the table before I could reply.

"They didn't—" I stopped as soon as I realized she couldn't hear me, and then a lurch rocked my stomach as the meal I'd just enjoyed suddenly wasn't sitting properly in my belly.

"Funderburke? Are you okay?"

"No. I need a minute. I need to check something in the car." I rushed back to my chair, pulled on my coat, and hurried out to the parking lot. Once inside my car, I dug the picture of me and Bertie that Zita had given me earlier that week out of my glove compartment. I'd left it there Monday afternoon, and with everything else going on, it'd completely slipped my mind until now.

I looked down at the photo of the two of us. We were both smiling, blissfully unaware of what the next few weeks would bring. Bertie's left arm was dangling over my shoulder, with the watch glinting on his wrist.

Once again, I lost all track of time, and I only snapped out of my reverie when Nerissa hopped into the passenger seat without my noticing her approaching the car. "Funderburke? What are you doing out here? It's been twenty minutes." She flipped back the collar tab of her black lambskin moto jacket, so it stopped tapping against her throat. "Why are you hiding from everybody?"

"I have a theory, and I really hope it's wrong."

"What?"

"I'll explain in a second. Would you please go back inside and ask Esme to meet us out here? Please? Over there, in that corner of the lot."

Nerissa didn't understand, but she nodded and left. I ambled out of the car. I was starting to enter a quasi-dream state, and it's amazing that I remembered to lock my car as I walked over to an empty spot a few yards from the back door to the restaurant. A moment later, Nerissa and Esme returned. The wind was picking up, and Nerissa, whose flowing hair was blowing parallel to the ground, zippered up her jacket, and Esme wrapped her worn tan cloth coat around herself tightly. "What's going on?" Esme asked.

"Have you ever seen any photographs of me and Bertie together as children before?"

"No. Mrs. Godspeed hid all of her old photos away. The memories are too much for her. I've seen one or two pictures of Bertie, but none of the two of you."

"She gave me this one recently." I held out the picture, using my hand to cover the part with the watch on Bertie's wrist. "Have you ever seen this before tonight?"

"No. Should I have? It's a nice one."

"Are you sure?"

"Uh-huh. Why?"

"It's the only picture of me and Bertie together that I know of, aside from some group shots in the Cuthbertson yearbooks. Have you ever seen our old yearbooks?"

"Definitely not. Funderburke, why are you acting so weird?"

"You're absolutely positive you never saw any old photos of me as a kid?"

"Yes."

"Did you ever read the police report of Bertie's murder or see any crime scene or autopsy photos?"

"What? No, gross. Why are you asking about that?"

"Esme, a little while ago, you said that the Godspeeds had given me my watch."

"Right. It was Bertie's, so I figured they'd wanted you to have it."

Nerissa made a sound that was half-gasp, half-hiccup. She'd started down the train of thought I'd been barreling along, and she didn't like the destination any more than I did. She slipped her hands into her pockets, and her slender frame started shivering like a sapling in a gale, but I suspected it was from more than just the chill in the air.

"What made you think it was Bertie's?" I asked, using every ounce of my strength to keep my voice calm.

"Well, he was wearing it…." Esme's voice trailed off, and the knot in my stomach kept getting tied increasingly tighter.

"Where did you see him wearing it? Because it wasn't his watch. It was mine. My late grandfather gave it to me, and after Bertie helped me one terrible night, I told him I wanted him to hold onto it for a while. He wore it for two weeks. Then he was killed."

I have never seen Nerissa's face turn so deathly pale before or since. Esme's facial muscles weren't moving at all, but there was something indescribable in her eyes that made me want to scream. But I didn't. Somehow I managed to talk just as I ordinarily did. "When we were twelve or thirteen, it wasn't like today, when people take a hundred photos of themselves a week with their phones. Ever since I first met you when we were both eighteen and I started volunteering at Bertie's Buddies, you've told me and the Godspeeds that you never met Bertie, that you never heard of Bertie until his family started the charity. Mrs. Godspeed hid the photos of Bertie for years because it hurt too much to look at them. I think this is the only photo of Bertie taken during the time he wore my grandfather's watch." I held out the framed photograph. Esme wouldn't look at it, so I held it right in front of her face. "The only photograph of him when he was wearing the watch. And it's been hidden away for years. You've never seen it."

I took at least seven long, deep breaths. "You didn't go to Cuthbertson, you weren't a friend of Bertie's, you never looked at this photograph before a few seconds ago, you didn't read the case file. What. Made. You. Think. This. Was. His. Watch?" I moved the photograph away and held my wrist up to her face. Her eyes glanced at the watch and immediately looked away. "It's a distinctive watch, with the coin, the notched band...I can see it would make an impression in people's memories. I've worn it in front of you dozens of times. I never told you how I got it. Yet you thought it was originally Bertie's. No reason why you would know the history of how it was worn by my grandfather, then me, then Bertie, and then me again. I've never seen fit to go into those details with you. But you got the ownership wrong, which means you never knew the true story. You just assumed. You saw Bertie wearing the watch at some point during the two weeks he had it. Not in this photograph, and no other image of him with the watch exists. He wasn't wearing it during his funeral. The police didn't return the watch to the Godspeeds for some time after he was buried, and they gave it back to me right after that."

I swallowed, searched her face for any expression that I could grab hold of, and pushed forward. "I do know of one other person who could've seen Bertie wearing the watch. In that grainy VHS security tape of the murder, you can see his killer running up to him, crouching down, tugging at his arm in what I now realize was an attempt to pull the watch off his lifeless wrist. It's a tricky clasp, you can't take it off easily unless you know exactly what to press and how. The killer gave up and ran away. You can't get a good look at the watch in the video. Bertie's completely off-screen, except for a bit of his hand when the killer was fiddling with the watch. But the shooter must have gotten a good look at the watch, and it stayed in the murderer's mind all of these years. I almost said "his" mind. Ever since I heard the news about the shooting, I always thought that the killer was a "he." Never for one moment did I consider that the hooded, faceless figure on that old VHS tape was a woman. Not even a grown woman. A girl Bertie's age."

Nerissa was shaking even more violently, and Esme wasn't moving at all.

"Tell me I'm wrong, Esme. Tell me I'm crazy. Please. You have no idea how much I want you to deny it. I desperately want you to assure me that everything I'm suggesting is some ridiculous fever dream." She said nothing.

She didn't even blink. "Please. We've been friends for a very long time. I've never known you to be anything other than an exemplary human being. This doesn't make sense to me. It doesn't fit what I know about the woman I've known and grown to deeply respect over all these years. I need to know that what I'm thinking is nonsense, brought about by not enough sleep and a ton of stress. Just look me in the eye and tell me I'm wrong. Scream at me, yelling how dare I accuse you of this. Slap me across the face and call me filthy names. Say this is a betrayal of our friendship. Give me another way you could have seen that watch. Anything. It doesn't matter how ludicrous. Tell me there's a photo or a video that I'm not aware of. Tell me you bumped into Bertie at a sandwich shop a week before he died, commented on his watch, and never knew that you'd actually met him until now, when you finally saw his photograph. I am so desperate to hear you deny this that if you tell me you jumped into a time machine that got abandoned in an alley and went back and saw Bertie wearing the watch, then I'll believe you."

Esme continued to say nothing. She just stared off into the distance, unable to meet my eyes.

A recent memory floated through my mind, and I rapidly did a bit more mental arithmetic. "And there's more… This photograph I'm holding is the only one that you've ever seen of me as a kid, isn't it? On the way up to Green Bay this week, you told me, "you've completely trimmed down since you were a kid." But we never met until I was a svelte eighteen-year-old. How did you know that I was heavy when I was younger? Did we cross paths before then without my knowing it?"

Tears were flowing down Esme's cheeks. She spoke in a barely audible whisper. I had to strain to hear her over the increasingly strong wind. "The funeral… I slipped inside the back of the church. I got there just as they were introducing you as you gave your eulogy. That's when I saw you for the first time. I remembered you when we were introduced a little over five years later. "Funderburke" is a memorable name…."

"You went to the funeral? Why?"

"I felt so guilty…I wanted to confess…but I didn't have the courage. I ran out right after your eulogy. I was so scared. I didn't want to go to jail."

Nerissa was still quivering. "It's true, then? Why? For the love of God, why?"

Esme flopped to her knees, threw herself against the chain-link fence next to us, and emitted an ear-piercing howl. It lasted nearly half a minute. I think people heard her primal scream in the next zip code.

"I didn't mean to do it!" she wailed, and every sentence she spoke was punctuated by sobs. "I had to get away. I told you! It was awful in those foster homes. The other kids were nasty, the adults smacked us for no reason. I had to get out of there. I thought if I could get some money, I could run off and go somewhere far away. One of the guys at the home had a gun. He showed it to us one day, saying he found it in an alley. He said there weren't any bullets in it, but he knew where to get some. The next day, when he was out smoking with some of his horrible friends, I took the gun, pulled on a hooded sweatshirt and another girl's sunglasses, and ran a few blocks down the street until I found what looked like an empty store. I must have been mad. I know it didn't make any sense, but I'd already been beaten up three times that week, and I was afraid it was going to get even worse, so I thought I had to get out as soon as I could.

When I chose that store, I thought the shopkeeper was the only one there. I pointed the gun at him and asked for all his money, but then he just collapsed from fright. I had no idea what to do. I was even thinking I should call for an ambulance when I heard a clatter off to one side. Bertie'd accidentally knocked over something. I didn't know he was there. I wasn't thinking straight. I just responded. I pulled the trigger without even realizing what I was doing. I didn't want to shoot him. I'd never even fired a gun before. The bullet should have gone wild. But it hit him. I don't know how it happened, it should've missed, but it hit him." Her sobs grew even louder. "I couldn't believe it. I never wanted it to happen. I thought the gun was empty. I took that boy's word for it. I was sure it was empty."

"There must have been one bullet in the chamber," I muttered. I glanced at my watch, and I felt the anger rising in me. "So you didn't mean to do it. But I saw the video. You ran over and tried to take this watch from him. You weren't so sorry that you were ready to run away empty-handed, were you?"

"I never tried to take the watch!" Esme shrieked. "I was checking for a pulse! I thought maybe he'd be okay. When I saw he wasn't...I ran. I sprinted back to the house, I put the gun and the sunglasses back where I found them, and I rushed into the bathroom and threw up for the rest of the night. My foster mother screamed and went at me with her belt because of the mess I made."

I was too furious to feel any sympathy. "And what? You figured that beating was punishment enough?"

Esme finally managed to look up at me. "I've been punishing myself ever since. I've never had a boyfriend because I don't believe I deserve to be loved. The next five years after it happened, I just accepted every bit of awfulness I endured at the homes, because I thought it was justice. But I'm so scared of prison. Don't you understand? The thought of being trapped with violent criminals and being unable to escape...I just thought that I could do a better job punishing myself than any court could. And when I found out that the Godspeeds had started a charity, I knew I had to volunteer there. I lied to you about why I started working there. I thought it was my best shot at redemption."

My self-control was totally gone. I was flailing my arms like a madman and screaming at the top of my lungs. "You worked for them all those years! You insinuated yourself into their lives, you became their right-hand woman, and you never stopped the pain they had from never knowing who took their son away from them!"

"You have to understand! The Godspeeds were so nice to me. They treated me like their own daughter. If I told them... Can you imagine the looks on their faces when they learned the truth? I couldn't take it! I just couldn't bear to see the horror in their eyes when they found out I killed Bertie!"

A short shriek came from behind us. I turned around and saw the Godspeed family, Mrs. Zwidecker, a bunch of other people from the party and other tables, and some of the waitstaff standing outside on the restaurant patio, staring at us. "We heard screaming..." one waitress mumbled.

There are no words to describe the expressions that Mr. and Mrs. Godspeed were making. As for Zita, the best metaphor I can use would be "a cyclone of fury." She rushed towards us, making a deafening yell, threw herself on Esme, and began pummeling her without mercy. Esme made no attempt to defend herself. Nerissa and everybody else watching assured me that I didn't say a word, but in my mind, I was thinking, "Harder! Harder!" so many times that I was sure I'd been audibly cheering Zita on in her punching. I'm ashamed of those feelings, but that's what was resonating in my mind, and I don't like bowdlerizing anything about myself. I don't know how long it lasted. Probably not more than ten or fifteen seconds later, Nerissa grabbed Zita and tried to pull her off of Esme, only to get a fist in her own eye for her troubles.

Nerissa's yelp of pain was enough to bring me out of my stupor. "Hey! What have you done!" I managed to pin Zita's arms to her sides and lift her up in the air. I held her at arm's length so she couldn't kick my chest and pointed her in Nerissa's direction. "Look what you did to Nerissa! Look at her!" My girlfriend's face had a big red mark on it. She'd have a nasty black eye soon.

The sight of the welt sobered up Zita. "I'm sorry," she blubbered, and burst into tears.

Everybody on the patio started hurrying towards us. Esme yelped, scrambled to her feet, and sprinted towards her car. By the time I handed Zita to Mr. Godspeed and ran after her, it was too late, and Esme was speeding off into the night. I stood on the curb, watching her car lights fade in the distance, trying to drive the thoughts of violent revenge from my head.

I probably stood there for at least a minute, until I felt a hand pressing on my shoulder. I turned and saw Nerissa's battered face looking up at me. "C'mon, Funderburke. Let's go inside."

Wrapping my arms around her, I pulled her as tightly as I could to my chest and held her there until I regained the power of speech. "I'll ask the waitress for a raw steak."

"And some ice cream," Nerissa said with a smile that didn't show up in her eyes. "I could use some."

Chapter Ten

Requiem

Not surprisingly, the tone of the party shifted dramatically from that point onwards. Most of the other guests made their exits within five minutes. As I helped Nerissa up the stairs and back into the restaurant, one of the waitresses asked me, "Should we call the police or something?" It was an excellent question, and I immediately phoned a friend of mine who's a homicide investigator. It took a little convincing to assure him that I wasn't pulling a prank on him, but eventually, he came to believe that I was telling the truth about Bertie's murder being solved, and he assured me that he was going to put out an APB for Esme and her car.

As it turned out, there was a rather large bachelor party in a different dining room at the restaurant, and there appeared to be a contest to see who could eat the most red meat. It would have been fun to be able to participate, but it meant that there was no raw steak available for Nerissa's eye. We made do with an ice pack made from a sealable plastic bag, a handful of cubes, and a clean napkin. After Nerissa's arm got tired, I held it to her eye for her. When a large scoop of chocolate ice cream arrived for her, she consumed two small spoonfuls, pushed the bowl over to me, and told me to finish it, and after I'd enjoyed a little, she took it back and ate two more spoonfuls before shoving it back in front of me and telling me to polish it off before she ate it all, and not to worry about getting an ice cream headache from rapid eating. I was happy to oblige. The dessert provided a much-needed distraction from…well, everything.

There wasn't much in the way of conversation, aside from recounting the events of everything that happened in the parking lot to the Godspeeds and Mrs. Zwidecker and filling in a few gaps for them. As soon as all of their questions were answered, Mrs. Godspeed placed her hand to her head.

"I have a terrible migraine. I need to go home right now."

The rest of her family appeared to be in no hurry to stay, so they pulled on their jackets. "Apologize to Nerissa again, sweetie," Mr. Godspeed told his daughter.

"I already said I was sorry three times," Zita replied.

"Well, say it again and keep apologizing until her eye is back to normal."

After a brief pout, Zita turned to Nerissa. "I'm sorry I hit you. I didn't mean to do it."

"No, you were trying to hit Esme."

"You know she deserved it."

"Don't ever strike anybody ever again unless your life is in danger," Mr. Godspeed warned his daughter.

"I won't."

"You'd better not, kid." Nerissa pushed my ice-pack-holding hand away, leaned forward, and hugged Zita. "It could've been worse. If you'd scuffed or scratched or torn my outfit, there'd be hell to pay."

It was lucky that Nerissa couldn't see that when she'd hugged Zita, Zita's fingers were still smeared with the remains of her dessert, and she had left a smudge of whipped cream on the back of Nerissa's jacket. I discreetly wiped it off with a napkin, and fortunately, no stain remained afterwards.

As the Godspeeds walked out the door, I was seized by a paralyzing fear that I was going to be stuck with the check. Fortunately, our waitress assured us that everything was taken care of, as Tyler Coquina had left a credit card number on file and insisted that all charges be billed to him. I wondered what his game was, and then decided to take full advantage of it, whatever it was. I ordered a bunch of easily-prepared items for carry-out after being assured that Tyler would be on the hook for every last meatball.

I couldn't believe that I'd been worried about the restaurant bill. By rights,

I should have been thinking about the revelation of who Bertie's killer was. My only explanation for worrying about money is that I was currently in a state of quasi-denial, as my brain was having difficulty processing the fact that I finally knew who was responsible for Bertie's death, along with the truth about who the culprit was. I'd dreamed about this moment for more than half my life, and now that I finally had the answers I wanted, I couldn't quite believe them, even though I knew they were true. This whole revelation was a lot less satisfying than I'd fantasized it being.

Eventually, I loaded four enormous paper bags filled with food into the trunk of my car, and Nerissa and Mrs. Zwidecker, and I rode off in science. When I went inside the Kaimings' house with Nerissa, I expected that the big focus would be on the three bags of Italian food I was lugging in (the fourth was still in the car, meant for my personal use), followed by my declaration that the Kaimings' Sunday dinner would be courtesy of Tyler Coquina. My mind was clearly not operating at peak condition, as I was briefly surprised by the fact that Keith and Midge were a lot less interested in the free food than in Nerissa's face, where the bruise was starting to develop.

"You should see the other girl," Nerissa quipped before she told me not to keep Mrs. Zwidecker waiting in the car, and that she'd tell her parents everything.

When we got back home, Mrs. Zwidecker surprised me by following me to her guest house.

"What's going on?"

"I'm going to make sure you take care of yourself tonight," she informed me. Over my objections, she tugged my walking coat off me, and gestured towards the bathroom. "Go in there and clean up for bed. You'll feel better after a shower."

"It's only eleven o'clock."

"And no good will come from your staying up and stewing. Do as I say. I'll put your food away."

I argued for another couple of minutes, then complied because I was exhausted and not because I was meekly following orders. When I came out with mildly damp hair and dressed in my sleepwear, Mrs. Zwidecker pushed a mug of warm Ovaltine into my hands. "Drink it and brush your teeth."

"Stop treating me like I'm five."

"I don't want you staying up, getting angrier, and then going out in search of Esme."

"I wasn't going to do that." At least, not before Mrs. Zwidecker put that idea in my head.

"Drink your Ovaltine and brush your teeth."

"Have we gone back in time two decades? Why are you acting like I'm a recalcitrant child?"

"Because I can see that things aren't right with you, and frankly, I've been worried sick about you ever since this whole situation started. You've either been sleeping all day or barely at all, you've been skipping meals, something I've never known you to do before, you lost all track of time in the pool, I haven't seen you go out and do anything purely for fun, and oh yes, you've been howling at the top of your lungs in the middle of the night with a nightmare! And if the next words out of your mouth are "I'm fine," you might just have to look for alternative living arrangements!"

I sipped Ovaltine. "You'd miss me."

"Yes, I would. So be sensible. You are obsessing, and when you obsess, you lose track of everything that makes you happy. When was the last time you read for fun or played a game, or even watched television? When did you most recently call a friend just to say hello or put on music?" I took a few minutes to think, and my train of thought was interrupted by Mrs. Zwidecker, "It was before you heard about Bertie's identity being stolen, wasn't it? A week and a half ago?"

"I suppose."

"You're not the only one who can scrutinize people and notice telling points about them. Your shaving's been haphazard. You've missed two spots on your throat and one under your left ear. You've taken in your belt a notch tighter than usual. And the T-shirt you're wearing is backwards."

I looked down and noticed the tag sticking out under my chin. Pulling my arms out of my sleeves and rotating it a hundred and eighty degrees, I fixed the problem. "Anything else?"

"You've been doing a terrible job of brushing your hair, but you never spend much time on that. I suppose that isn't out of the ordinary. But you forgot to unplug your charging cords from that power strip over there. You always take them out because you're worried that they might be a fire hazard."

She was right. I yanked out the cords.

"Finish your Ovaltine and brush your teeth."

"How long are you going to treat me like a child?"

"When are you going to go back to normal?"

"When this whole case is resolved."

"What do you consider 'resolved'?" When Esme's caught? When she's convicted? That could take months, maybe more than a year. Are you going to go on no sleep one night, fourteen hours the next for all that time? Are you going to swim across Lake Michigan and back every weekend? When are you going to take Nerissa out and have an evening of fun with your friends?"

"I'm a little suspicious of all my friends now. One person I really cared about and respected turned out to have been the killer of my childhood best pal. I wonder what secrets my other buddies are hiding."

"Now you're being sulky and irritable. You need to get some sleep."

"First, I need to check—"

"Brush your teeth first."

I'm not sure why I didn't make a fuss. I just put down the mug and took care of my personal hygiene. When I came back from the bathroom, I saw that she was stuffing my wi-fi router into her purse. "What are you doing with that?"

"I'm confiscating it for the night, along with your cell phone, your tablet, and your car keys. I want you to rest without technological distractions. And turn off all of your alarms. Get as much sleep as you can."

"I have to be up for church."

"You can go to the four o'clock Mass tomorrow afternoon. I have a feeling that you'll be getting another one of your marathon slumbers tonight."

I started yawning. "Did you put something in my Ovaltine?"

"No. I suspect all of your adrenaline has just run out, and you're starting to crash. Get into your bed now."

My attempt to object was thwarted by another massive yawn, and my pillows and mattresses looked so warm and comfortable, I found myself climbing in and pulling the covers over me. "Aren't you going to tuck me in and read me a story?"

Mrs. Zwidecker straightened out my sheets and blanket. "Once upon a time, there was a boy named Isaiah Funderburke. He was very intelligent, and he cared a lot about getting justice and writing wrongs, but he had a problem. When he got too wrapped up in a case, he lost track of many of the ordinary things in his life. People who cared about him started worrying. His girlfriend came to his former teacher on a couple of occasions, and told her that she'd never seen her boyfriend so obsessed over something. She said her parents had noticed how distracted he was, too. Even her daughter and some of her little siblings thought that something was wrong with Isaiah, and came to his former teacher as well to express their concern. So did a lot of his co-workers. His former teacher tried to make him realize that he had to spend less time trying to wrap up the details of the case and more time trying to figure out how to go back to his normal, balanced mindset, because he'd never live happily ever after until he was ready to close the case and start focusing on the living people who cared about him, rather than fixating on the one dear friend of his who was dead. The end."

"I hate those stories with the preachy, didactic morals," I informed Mrs. Zwidecker as she shut off the light and opened the door.

"Oh, hush. But say your bedtime prayers first," she replied as she turned the lock.

"I want a glass of water, please," I called out as she shut the door and twisted the handle to make sure it was locked. She didn't reply. I didn't really want water. I just needed to get in the last word.

After my regular nighttime prayer routine, I planned to just lie quietly in bed until Mrs. Zwidecker went to sleep, and then turn on my computer and use my neighbor's wi-fi, which wasn't password protected, to try to figure out where Esme might be going, and use my spare car key in my desk to go out and search for her. I was not expecting to slip into unconsciousness so quickly. When I checked the glowing digits on my bedside clock right before shutting my eyes, it was a quarter past eleven at night. By the time my eyes finally opened, it was two forty-five in the afternoon.

I can hardly believe it myself, but when I climbed out of bed, the events of the previous night were completely out of my mind. A few minutes later, as I was emerging from the bathroom, I heard a key in my door and saw Mrs. Zwidecker entering with a tray with a generous slice of a frittata, toast, and fruit on it. "I'm glad you got a good rest, Isaiah. Eat quickly—you have to be at church in seventy minutes, and you want to be finished eating an hour beforehand."

After thanking her, I reached into the fridge to get myself some water and milk. As soon as I opened the door, I saw the boxes of takeout from the previous night, recalled everything, and promptly lost my appetite. Then I smelled that the frittata was my favorite—smoked salmon and Roquefort—and decided I was hungry after all. As I picked up my fork, Mrs. Zwidecker reminded me to say grace, and I did.

"Just eat quietly, and I'll do the talking," Mrs. Zwidecker said as she sat across from me at my little table in the corner. "Esme is in custody."

"They found her?"

"No. She turned herself in. Not long after she left the restaurant, she stopped at a coffee shop, bought herself a drink, and a little later, a pair of uniformed officers entered. Just as they were about to leave, she walked up to them and confessed."

"You're kidding me."

"Did you think she'd be across the Canadian border by now?"

"The possibility crossed my mind, yes."

"She has gotten a lawyer—I assume the authorities found her a public defender—even though she appears to be willing to accept whatever sentence they give her."

"Good."

"She just had one request. She wants to talk to you."

"Hard pass."

"I understand your feelings." From the tone of her voice, it was clear that she wanted me to accept Esme's request, and I told her I detected that implication.

"That's right, Isaiah."

"Weren't you the one who gave the big speech last night about moving on and putting all of this behind me? Well, I'm letting go. And the best way to do it is to completely write off the person who caused this. I'm walking away. I'm passing up the chance to wallow. Instead of obsessing, I'm going to focus on the people I care about and helping my students, and doing some good in the world. That's what you want, right?" Feeling like I'd made my point, I speared another morsel of frittata with my fork and consumed it with an expression I hoped reflected triumph and defiance.

Mrs. Zwidecker poured herself a glass of water from the pitcher on the table and drank it slowly. When she'd finished, she set it down and looked back up at me. "Isaiah, I'm not just your former teacher and your landlady. I'm also your godmother. You and I have no blood tie, but I believe we're family, and I know you feel the same way."

"No argument there."

"As your godmother, I have a duty to look after your spiritual welfare. I know what you believe in, and I know how hard you strive to be a good person. You're devoted to helping your students. You go to church at least twice a week, often more. Your relationship with Nerissa is beyond reproach. I could go on, but you don't need to be told what you're doing right. It's what you need to do differently that's the issue here."

"All right, what am I doing wrong?"

"Isaiah, a lot of people have done you wrong over the course of your life. Many of them are people who hurt you with a terrible betrayal, like your mother, your brother, your father—"

"My half-brother and my not-father."

"All right. Your stepfather. Various divorce lawyers and judges. Employers."

"A lot of others. I have a list."

"Exactly. You keep that list in your head, with everybody who's ever done you wrong on it, arranged in order of how badly they've harmed you, with every cruelty and snub listed in chronological order. You read that list a dozen times a day, and you pick the wounds and never let them heal."

"It's not that I don't want the wounds to heal. It's that I just can't make the indignation go away."

"Isaiah, I think I phrased my thoughts badly last night. If you're ever going to get through the problems and terrible memories that cause you so much pain–"

"I am not in pain."

"We'll quibble over my choice of words later. The point is that you need to work on forgiveness."

I scraped the last of the frittata from my plate and deposited it in my mouth. When I'd swallowed it, I replied, "That's what Uncle Francis says. It's not that I don't try. Every week, I tell myself, this is it, I'm done with all of this, I forgive these people. And then a few days later, the memory of the iniquity comes back tenfold, and I'm back where I started. Uncle Francis tells me that it's like quitting smoking. You have to keep trying and trying until it finally takes permanently."

"That's sound advice."

"It would be a lot easier if one of them actually had the guts to come to me, collapse to the ground, and apologize for all the wrongs they've done me while washing my feet with their salty tears."

"Well, I don't know if any of your family members will ever show up hats in hands with genuine regret in their hearts. But it just so happens that there is one person who's done something horrible to you and people you deeply care about, and she wants to do something to make it right. Is there anybody else in your life who's done something dreadful to you, who now wants to talk it over with you, knowing that there's no justification for what she did, but that she needs to take the first steps to make it right, even though there are some actions that can never be taken back? I can think of one other person who's done you wrong, and you're still furious with her."

"Very true."

"At least you're consistent in your burning fury. You may not have forgiven the people in your life who've wronged you, but you've never forgiven yourself, either."

"I'll forgive myself when I've earned it."

"When will that be?"

"I'll know when it happens."

"Maybe you'll have a better idea of what you need to do when you take steps towards forgiving Esme."

"It's not like she's going to suffer much for what she did."

"What makes you say that, Isaiah?"

"If she tells the story she told me, she probably won't get charged with anything worse than involuntary manslaughter or something along those lines. Plus the fact that she was very much a child herself when it happened, give or take a year, and that she turned herself in and the only real evidence is her own confession, if her lawyer's even half-decent, it's unlikely she'll spend much time in prison."

"Do you think that she deserves to suffer?"

"Bertie's dead. What do you think?"

"You and I have both met some terrible people in our time. Sociopaths and liars and criminals who feel no remorse."

"Human scum."

"Is Esme a monster?"

I knew the answer, I just needed a little time to gather up the strength to say it. "No."

"We saw her screaming last night. I think she's been wrestling with her conscience for a very long time."

"A decade and a half of wrestling, and she didn't do anything about it until last night."

"She did do something. She volunteered at the Godspeeds' charity and lived an exemplary life." Mrs. Zwidecker paused. "I think there's something else that bothers you so much about her being the killer."

"That I considered her a friend?"

"That you two were so much alike." That comment left me speechless, and Mrs. Zwidecker kept going. "You both had a rough time of it at thirteen. Both of you came up with a plan to get out of your current situation. Not very smart plans, terrible plans. Horribly misguided, shocking plans from otherwise intelligent people."

"Can you blame me for not thinking clearly?"

"No, but what if things had gone very differently? What if your stepfather had a gun, and you decided to use it on yourself, only to pull away at the last second, and the bullet went soaring through the window and hit some innocent person? Or if you'd been on that cliff, and you'd fumbled about on the edge and sent a rock hurtling down, and it just happened to hit some person out for a walk on the beach below?"

"There was deep water directly under that cliff. No one could walk on it aside from Jesus."

"But you get my meaning."

"Of course I do. You're not exactly being subtle here."

"Perhaps not."

"But you're forgetting one thing. Yeah, I know that Esme had a terrible time of it as a kid. I know she didn't mean to do it. She was desperate, she was scared, she never wanted it to happen, I get all that. But strip all of that away, and there's one point left that you can't escape. *She killed Bertie.* If it were a stranger, it'd be so much easier to make excuses, not that it would be right to do so, but dammit, it was Bertie!"

Mrs. Zwidecker said nothing for a few moments. "Isaiah, I've seen how passionate you are about your job as the Student Advocate. If the shooting took place today instead of half your lifetime ago, if you didn't know the victim, and if thirteen-year-old Esme went to Cuthbertson and came to you crying, begging for help, what would you do then?"

I didn't have an answer for that. I needed time to think about that, and said so. Mrs. Zwidecker saw the wisdom in letting me think it out, and took away the breakfast dishes without further comment.

"I want my cell phone and everything else back, please," I informed her, and two minutes later, she was back with everything she'd taken the previous night.

By the time I'd gone through all my voicemail messages and emails, most of them connected to last night, my earlier exhaustion came flowing back, and I was in no mood to relive the previous evening mentally. Nerissa was on her way to pick me and Mrs. Zwidecker up for church, and I had just enough time to get myself shaved and dressed when Nerissa knocked on my door, wearing a loose-fitting grey turtleneck sweater, a long and glossy black skirt, a candy-apple red leather knee-length coat with matching boots, and a thick pair of sunglasses. She removed the last of these items as I opened the door, revealing an eye that looked almost—but not quite—normal.

"Pretty skillful makeup job there, Kaiming."

"Thanks. I learned the basics of covering up bruises from my birth mother when I was eleven, when she was dating a political activist and self-described male feminist. Thank God I didn't have to use the skills I picked up from one of our precious few mommy-daughter moments until now."

"I should have prevented it from happening."

"Please. I'm a big girl, and I can take care of myself. A lot of the time. Since we've been dating, you've had my back against biker gangs, homeless people suffering from mental illness, street criminals, grabby-handed middle-aged men with tight-lipped wives, wild boars, and feral cats. I figured I could handle an emotionally devastated thirteen-year-old girl on my own. Live and learn."

"So we're good?"

"We're great. I'm more concerned about you."

We talked in the car, and not once did I use the words "Fine" or "Okay." After Mass, I had a few more quick words with Uncle Francis.

"Do you blame me for not wanting to see Esme?"

"No. But I do want you to think about one question. How would Bertie want you to proceed from here?"

"That is emotional blackmail."

"No, it's a spiritual exercise."

"Po-TAY-to, po-TAH-to."

"And one more thing. There's another woman you need to speak to, besides Esme."

"No."

"She's quite determined to speak to you."

"I gave her plenty of chances, and now she's out."

165

"Matthew 18:22."

"Are you and Mrs. Zwidecker tag-teaming me on forgiveness?"

"Do you think we'd try anything like that if we didn't think it was of critical importance for you?"

"I can only take so much. Maybe I could handle Esme or her, but not both in the same year."

"Just keep praying on it, Isaiah. And prepare yourself. I have a feeling that if you don't call her, she'll find a way to make you talk to her."

"Forewarned is forearmed."

"Isaiah?" Uncle Francis called out as I turned to walk away. "I know you don't have as much of a family as you'd like, and none of that's your fault, but you should never give up on a family member if you can help it."

I smiled at him. "I'm just grateful for the little bit of *real* family that I have."

"You have a lot of people who care about you, Isaiah. Keep thinking about why that is."

At the time, other issues filled my mind besides my popularity. My meal with the Kaimings that evening tasted even better when I remembered who unknowingly paid for it. I found myself wishing I could be there when he opened up his credit card bill. Afterwards, Keith took me aside into his study.

"You, too?" I asked him as I shut the door.

"What do you mean?"

"Mrs. Zwidecker. Uncle Francis. Everybody's lining up to tell me to talk to Esme."

"No one's told me to pass a message on to you. I want to talk to you about something else. Toby was talking to me the other day, and I thought I should address this issue with you."

"Oh?"

"You know that Toby refers to Midge and me as "Yen-Yen" and "Yeh-Yeh." That's Chinese for "paternal grandmother and father." At the time, both of them were still under forty. Keith didn't mind at all. Midge wasn't quite as thrilled, but she went with it because of how much she loved the kid and Nerissa.

"Yes."

"She asked me how I thought you'd respond to her calling you "Dad." He probably heard the thud as my heart went hurtling down towards my feet. "She doesn't—and I don't either—want to put pressure on you and Nerissa and your relationship. But it's something you should be aware of and prepared for, and I know from experience how this can throw you for a loop. I know how fond you are of Toby, and she adores you, and..."

Nothing else Keith said registered for the next few minutes. I had too much going on between my ears. I'd always wanted a family of my own, but the thought of actually having a kid refer to me as "Dad" sent an electric shock through me, especially a teenager. When I brought this point up with Keith later, he reiterated that he'd had a very similar reaction a bit over a decade earlier when Nerissa had come to him and asked her to adopt her.

It made a difference in a way I'm not sure how to explain. This burning knot of anger in my gut that I'd been carrying around was starting to untie, as I started fretting about what sort of example I'd be setting for my own kids by teaching them that some people deserved not to be forgiven. I don't want to replicate my entire thought process. I just know when I left the Kaimings that night, my mind was in a very different place than it was a couple of hours earlier. It's one thing when you can tell yourself that your grudges and rage are your own private business. I know from personal experiences of watching scores of acrimonious divorces that loathing can be passed down from one generation to the next. Did I want my first gift to my stepdaughter to be a white-hot, seething hatred for Esme?

Before I left that night, I had a conversation with Toby in Nerissa's presence. It's one of the most personal and powerful talks I've ever had, and I'm not comfortable sharing the details right now. I've tried to provide as many details as possible in this narrative, but some things you just have to keep to yourself.

I will say that prior to that conversation, Toby had always referred to me as "Funderburke." After that night, she never called me that again. And I couldn't be happier.

On Monday, my mindset was very different. Hearing Toby refer to me by a new moniker had altered my mindset in ways I couldn't explain. I knew that if I ever saw Esme again, I wouldn't be hugging her and telling her that everything was okay But I no longer wished to see her in the electric chair and pull the switch myself. That was progress, I supposed.

Around ten-thirty, two visitors arrived at my office. I welcomed the Godspeeds, and asked what they were doing there.

"We're here to take you to a meeting," Mr. Godspeed informed me.

"Where—" I didn't finish that question. I knew. "I'm not ready yet."

"Neither are we," Mrs. Godspeed replied. "Nevertheless, we have an appointment to speak with Esme and her lawyer at eleven, and we want you to be there. We *need* you there, Isaiah. We need you to be our rock this morning."

"What does she hope to gain by this?" It wasn't a charitable question on my part, but I was suspicious, and I had no filter.

"I don't know who her lawyer is, but whoever it is isn't your average public defender. Esme's attorney must be pretty well-connected and is taking the case pro bono."

"What?" This was weird on countless levels. Why would some high-powered lawyer take a case where the killer had confessed? What would be the point? Did the lawyer have some ulterior motive connected to the case? "That makes no sense."

"We're confused, too. Apparently, this lawyer has enough pull to talk to prosecutors on a Sunday and work out a tentative deal." Mr. Godspeed repeated the reasons I'd thought of earlier as to why Esme might receive a light sentence. "The D.A.'s office has a stipulation before they go forward with the deal. They want to talk to us. If we agree, they'll move forward."

"I don't like this one bit," I muttered.

"We're not thrilled either, but what are our options? There's no tangible evidence against her. If she says she was joking or something like that…."

"She turned herself in," I reminded Mr. Godspeed.

"I hear that her lawyer is suggesting that it was all a mini-breakdown due to stress. It's either a few years at a minimum-security prison or…."

"Or nothing," I finished.

"Would that be so terrible?" Mrs. Godspeed asked. "All these years, we didn't know who shot Bertie. We gave up on ever learning the truth. A decade ago, I told myself it didn't matter if the killer was punished or not, I just wanted to know. Then I made my peace with never knowing. Now I do, and I wish I didn't."

"I still can't believe it." Mr. Godspeed shuddered, and then brought his palm down flat on my desk with a slap that shook all the items on it.

"If we're going to make it to our appointment, we're going to have to leave right now," Mrs. Godspeed informed me. "Please, come with us."

And I did. My next couple of hours were clear, so there was no convincing excuse to stay at work. We arrived at the facility at two minutes to eleven, and we were led into a waiting room, where Esme's lawyer was expecting us. I didn't even enter the room. As soon as I saw who was waiting for us, I turned around. "Goodbye," I said at the top of my lungs.

"Isaiah! Come back here!"

I didn't answer the lawyer's call, or the Godspeeds' either. I was halfway down the corridor when I heard high-heeled shoes clicking along the floor. "Isaiah! Do not make me chase after you!"

I wasn't sure why I stopped walking. I felt a hand on my shoulder, and I whirled around. "Let go of me," I snapped at Michelle Lilith.

"Please, listen to what I have to say."

"Why are you doing this? Why did you take this case? Did you do it just to mess with me? This is Bertie! You knew him! The fact that you did this proves that you are the most twisted, inhuman—"

"Isaiah!" Mrs. Godspeed's voice reverberated down the hall. "I know you're angry at her. I know she's hurt you. But you cannot, must not talk to your mother that way!"

I said nothing and didn't move, either. A few moments later, Mrs. Godspeed spoke again, more softly this time, "Isaiah, as a favor to us, please, come inside and talk with us now. You can address your issues later, but right now, we need you here with us. Please."

All of the replies I wanted to make sounded so rage-filled in my head that I knew that no matter how much I wanted to say them, I mustn't. I shuffled into the room and accepted the chair that Mr. Godspeed drew out for me. Everyone else sat down as well, and momentarily a handcuffed, prison-uniformed Esme was led into the room.

The tears were still flowing down her cheeks. "I'm so sorry…" she mumbled over and over again. "I'm so sorry."

I hear that a lot, whether it's from students who've gotten caught doing something wrong and think a little fake contrition will get them off the hook, or parents who've been caught cheating, or criminals who think a few sniffles will keep them out of jail. I don't claim to be a human polygraph, but when I looked through Esme's teardrops and into her eyes, I saw no guile whatsoever, just genuine emotion and regret.

For more than half my life, a murdering monster who'd robbed my best friend of his future had haunted my nightmares. I had always imagined Bertie's killer as pure evil. Esme may not have been as good a person as I'd thought she was two days earlier, but I didn't believe there was anything cruel in her.

"Do you agree that everything said here is off the record?" my mother asked.

"No, I do not," was my flat reply. My mother's eyebrow arched, but the expression on her face made it clear that this was exactly what she'd expected from me.

"Esme, as your lawyer, I strongly advise you not to speak unless we get a promise that whatever you say here can never be repeated in court or any other legal setting."

"Your attorney's giving you good advice, Esme," I informed her. "Talk, please."

My mother made further objections, but she was interrupted when Esme blurted out, "Did you ever read *From the Mixed-Up Files of Mrs. Basil E. Frankweiler?*"

"I did," I replied as the others in the room looked confused. "It's a Newbery-Award-winning children's book about a pair of siblings who decided to run away from home and live at the Metropolitan Museum of Art," I explained to bring everybody else in the room up to speed.

"That's an odd place to run away to," Mrs. Godspeed commented.

"I believe that they sleep in antique beds on display, bathe in a big fountain, and collect coins from that fountain in order to buy food."

"Right," Esme nodded. "I hated living at the foster home. I was so miserable there. I had no friends, I was scared, and I knew I had to get away."

"Where were you planning to go? The Milwaukee Art Museum? The Milwaukee Public Museum?"

For the first time, Esme made a little smile due to my questions. "Disney World. I thought that if I could just raise a little money, I could take a bus down to Florida, buy a ticket, find places to hide and sleep, and just live there forever."

"How old were you?"

"Twelve. Nearly thirteen. It was stupid, there's no way I could've stayed there for more than a day or two without getting caught, but it was a crazy dream I'd had for years, and I was getting scared in the foster home. I just had to get away, and I thought if I robbed a few stores...."

I knew the rest. "So why are you doing this?"

"What do you mean?"

"Why are you making a deal? A person who takes a plea bargain is trying to get a lesser sentence than she would if she went to trial and got convicted. But no matter how little jail time you're getting under this plea, it's got to be more than nothing, which is what you'd get if you denied everything. There isn't one scrap of forensic evidence against you. You've got witnesses to your confession, but you can claim you were drunk and you didn't know what you were saying. It's too late to get a blood test to prove you had nothing but club soda all night. And what would happen if the Godspeeds said "no deal?" The D.A. would say "no case," and you'd be free to go. You have everything to lose and nothing to gain by this deal. You could walk right out of the courtroom and move to a new city with a fresh start."

"It doesn't matter," Esme whispered, staring at her own hands. "Whether this deal goes through or not, it's all the same."

"What do you mean by that?" Mr. Godspeed asked. "I don't understand."

"I do," I said as a flash of understanding zapped me. "She's planning to kill herself."

Three faces in the room looked shocked. The fourth looked up at me for a few moments before nodding.

"It's only right," Esme whispered.

"The hell it is." Mr. Godspeed spoke with surprising vehemence. "This is not how your story ends."

Esme looked up with exhausted eyes. "For more than half my life, I've been pretending that afternoon never happened. It was all a terrible dream. I tried to smother my conscience by performing acts of charity. It worked for a while. I almost convinced myself that I was a good person."

"Basically good people can do horrible things. It doesn't have to define the rest of their lives," Mrs. Godspeed told her. "I have already lost a son. I am not prepared to lose a daughter as well."

Esme quavered like a gelatin mold, and the crying started again. "Don't. Don't forgive me and tell me it's going to be okay. I can't take it." Her voice grew high and shrill. "I want to get out of here! I have to go now!"

A pair of guards appeared and gently led her away. "I want her under suicide watch! Do you hear me?" my mother said. The guards assured her that they'd make sure she'd be safe, and as she followed them, my mother, ever the legal pit bull, informed them if any harm came to her client, there'd be a lawsuit so severe that they'd have to melt down the cell bars for scrap to pay the settlement.

The Godspeeds looked utterly exhausted. "I have a terrible headache," Mrs. Godspeed groaned.

"That's not surprising," I said. "This is a really stressful time."

"It's more than that," Mrs. Godspeed continued. "Esme has been one of our rocks. Bertie's Buddies wouldn't be here if not for her. I'm not sure if I would be here if not for her."

"I know, but...how? How is it possible that you two aren't out for her blood?"

"I believe I put it pretty well, Isaiah. I've lost too much already. Losing more is not an option."

"There's something else," Mr. Godspeed added. "I need to believe that a stain can be washed clean, without so much as a mark remaining. Esme hurt us more deeply than I can express, but she's also helped heal our wounds as well."

"So you're okay towards her now?"

"No," Mr. Godspeed sighed. "But we deeply want to be."

"We're not going to be around forever," Mrs. Godspeed added. "We've hoped for a long time that Esme would run Bertie's Buddies after we retire. With luck, that could still happen. Keeping the charity going would be a far more useful way to spend her life than rotting away in a cell."

"Do you think you can convince her?"

Mr. Godspeed shrugged. "I'm not very skilled at persuasion. But you are."

"I am nowhere near where you two are in terms of viewing the rehabilitation of Esme."

"We know. But hopefully sometime soon you can get there. We're going to visit Esme as often as we can, and we'll write to her as well. We'd love it if you could send her letters a few times a week."

"And now," Mrs. Godspeed declared, "I have to go home. My head is about to explode." She was very shaky on her feet, and as she stumbled against the wall, I scooped her up and carried her all the way back to the car. "Isaiah," she whispered, "just so you know, Esme's not the only young person in my life not related to me who I still love like my own child."

My throat closed up and I was unable to speak for a while. As I eased her into her car seat, I recovered enough to say, "Your home is in the opposite direction from Cuthbertson. Go home as fast as you can. I'll get a ride-share back to school."

"My law offices are just a little bit north of Cuthbertson. I'll drive you there." I whirled around and saw my mother behind us.

"That's not necessary–"

"Let your mother give you a ride, Isaiah," Mr. Godspeed told me. He said it so firmly I would have felt like a churl to balk further.

And so, I found myself in my mother's Mercedes, trying to think of something pleasant to say and to keep my temper in check.

"Are you wondering why I volunteered to take Esme's case?" my mother queried.

"I was trying to find a polite way to ask. Surely you can't still be upset with the little boy who came to our house when we were nine and accidentally chipped one of your plates? Even you wouldn't hold a grudge so tightly you'd want to see his killer walk."

"No..." she said as her knuckles whitened. "I knew that if I represented her, even if the case didn't go to trial, I would very likely be able to take depositions with you and see you at hearings and everything else. Even with a plea, the next couple of weeks could bring a bunch of conversations with you."

"You wanted to see me in court?"

"I wanted to see you, period. When we ran into each other at my client's house a few days ago, I realized how much I missed you. I didn't think you'd see me willingly, so I thought if I could draw you into these legal proceedings–"

"You've always been more comfortable in a courtroom. God forbid you should actually try to approach someone like a normal person. You'd much rather use a subpoena than a telephone."

"I've been trying find the courage to call you for a very long time, but I've been afraid of how you might respond to me."

"Can you blame me? All those years ago, you should have believed me."

"I know I should have. You have to understand, I physically couldn't let myself accept that your brother was lying and it was your stepfather who was...."

"Go on, say it."

"I couldn't even consider it. I was expecting your sister—"

"Half-sister."

"—and I wouldn't let myself consider that my child on the way had the DNA of a monster in her."

"How is she, by the way?" At that time, I'd never had a proper conversation with my half-sibling, and we were total strangers.

"She's going through a very difficult time. Things are very strained at home."

"That's too bad."

"Your brother's not doing well, either. He's having a lot of issues."

"Half-brother. A guilty conscience will do that."

"I know he hurt you, but he suffered in ways that you, thank God, never had to endure."

She was right, and I didn't want to admit it, so I said nothing. After a while, she was the one who broke the silence. "How's Leather Girl?"

"Getting hotter and more awesome every day. Thank you for asking." I debated whether or not to continue and then said, "I think you're a grandmother now."

After my mother nearly hit a post box, I hastily added. "Not that way. Her daughter considers me her father now, so…."

"Oh, I see. I'd love to meet her someday. Do you think I'll ever get a dinner invitation at the Kaimings?"

"You'd have to ask them. It's their home."

"They'd invite me if you'd ask them. Would you, please?"

"I'll think about it."

"I want us to be a mother and son again, Isaiah."

"What is it about me that makes everybody want me to be part of their family?"

"What do I have to do, Isaiah?"

I paused. "You could fire your law librarian."

"Delia? Oh." She sighed. "Don't you think she's been punished enough?"

"She was instrumental in sending three decent men to jail for nonpayment of child support after she bankrupted them. She made a small fortune, and two young women committed suicide because of what she did to their families."

"That wasn't all on her. She's been disbarred. She's lost most of her money. She's nearly broke."

"Did she give it back to the people she took it from?"

"No, she made some bad investments."

"And you gave her a job to help her out. I remember. She's an old friend of yours."

"You keep seeing people you dislike as pure evil. Delia is not a villain."

"How many lives does someone have to destroy before you see her as the terrible person she is?"

By now, we were pulling into the Cuthbertson Hall parking lot. "Isaiah, I'm very proud of you, but as your mother, I have to warn you about all that anger you're carrying around. If you don't find a way to get rid of it—"

"I know. Terrible consequences, blah blah blah." As I climbed out of the car, I turned around and said, "Thank you for the advice. And the ride." Before I shut the door, I took a deep breath and added, "I'd like to get through this, but I need time."

"You've had about a decade and a half. What more do you want from me?"

"How about an apology?"

She looked down at her hands. "Apologizing is very difficult for me. If you promise to give our relationship another chance, will you give me time to find a way to express my... feelings?"

"Good luck with that." I shut the door and took two steps towards the school, and then something forced me to turn around and open the door again. "I'm not saying no. I'm just saying that right now, I need to process this whole Bertie and Esme situation. I'm being asked to forgive an awful lot right now, and I need to get my bearings."

"I understand. Perhaps I'm putting too much on you right now. But I've—we've—lost so much time already, please don't waste much more."

"I'll work on it." I closed the car door, took a breath, and then reopened it. "Goodbye, Mother."

That was both the end and the beginning. It was the end of Bertie's case, and it was also the end of the stage in my life when I was able to comfortably ignore everything that had wounded me in the past, and it was the beginning of a time when I was compelled to address people and issues that I thought I had safely written out of my life.

The saga of my relationship with my family—all the various branches of it—played out over the coming years, and this is not the place to address those matters. Thankfully, as I dealt with people I'd rather not have, I had a core of people I could trust to help me.

Nerissa, the Kaimings, Mrs. Zwidecker, Uncle Francis, and the Godspeeds were critical to helping me keep my head on straight as Esme's legal situation played out. My mother made sure that she got psychiatric care while in custody, and after the plea deal was accepted, she went away for a couple of years. Not long before, I would have considered it a slap on the wrist. Now, I considered it both too lenient and wholly unnecessary. On an intellectual level, I'd long understood that rehabilitation ought to be a critical part of the criminal justice system. Esme was never a cold-blooded killer, and I was certain that she'd never commit an act of violence again.

I started writing to her three times a week, and having little to do in prison, Esme always wrote back two times for every letter I sent her. I can't pinpoint the exact moment when I stopped feeling anger towards her and simply started viewing her as my longtime friend who'd made a terrible mistake half a lifetime ago, but after a few months, I started daydreaming about an alternative timeline where Bertie never died, Esme went to Cuthbertson, and Bertie and Esme wound up together, leading Nerissa and me to double-date with them a lot. Not for the first time, I realized that my fantasies were way better than reality.

Almost three months later, on the last day of the school year, there was a new installation in the Grove of Remembrance, which is my personal name for a collection of trees off to the side of the school. Every so often, someone has a sapling planted in honor of a deceased loved one, and a plaque is installed at the base of the tree with the late one's name and an additional message. Bertie's tree was paid for by an anonymous donor. It didn't take me long to figure out that my mother was behind it.

Even as many years have passed, as my own family has grown and my career has taken off in directions I could never have anticipated, I come out to the Grove of Remembrance and stand by Bertie's tree almost every day. I look down at the plaque that says, "BERTRAM "BERTIE" GODSPEED: BELOVED SON AND FRIEND," and every time I visit, I think of a different joyous memory the two of us shared. For many years, every time I thought of Bertie, I swore that someday I would get justice for him. Now that I've achieved that, when I stand by his tree, with the powerful Milwaukee winds blowing through my hair and making my coat billow, I focus on the happiness he brought me during the worst years of my life, and I walk back to my office and look at the picture of the two of us that's installed in a position of honor on my wall, and I thank him for his wonderful gift of friendship.

A Note From The Author

If you or someone you care about are in a crisis, please get help. Talk to a mental health professional, a member of the clergy, a family member, a friend, or call The National Suicide Prevention Lifeline at 1-800-273-8255, which is available for free all day, every day.

Acknowledgements

Special thanks to the Dames of Detection: Verena Rose, Harriette Sackler, and Shawn Reilly Simmons of Level Best Books for their belief in this book. As always, none of this would be possible without my parents Drs. Carlyle and Patricia Chan. I also need to thank all of my friends and teachers from the University School of Milwaukee.

About the Author

Chris Chan is a writer, educator and historian. He works as a researcher and "International Goodwill Ambassador" for Agatha Christie Ltd. His true crime articles, reviews, and short fiction have appeared in *The Strand*, *The Wisconsin Magazine of History*, *Mystery Weekly*, *Gilbert!*, Nerd HQ, Akashic Books' *Mondays are Murder* webseries, *The Baker Street Journal*, *The MX Book of New Sherlock Holmes Stories*, *Masthead: The Best New England Crime Stories*, *Sherlock Holmes Mystery Magazine*, and multiple Belanger Books anthologies. He is the creator of the Funderburke and Kaiming mysteries, a series featuring private investigators who work for a school and help students during times of crisis. The Funderburke short story "The Six-Year- Old Serial Killer" was nominated for a Derringer Award. His first book, Sherlock & Irene: The Secret Truth Behind "A Scandal in Bohemia," was publishedin 2020 by MX Publishing, and he is also the author of the comedic novel *Sherlock's Secretary*. His book *Murder Most Grotesque: The Comedic Crime Fiction of Joyce Porter* (Level Best Books) was nominated for the 2022 Agatha Award for Best Non-Fiction.

SOCIAL MEDIA HANDLES:
   Twitter: @GKCfan
   Facebook: https://www.facebook.com/chris.chan.7374/

AUTHOR WEBSITE:

Blog: https://chrischancrimeandcriticism.blogspot.com

Also by Chris Chan

Non-fiction literary criticism:

Sherlock & Irene: The Secret Truth Behind "A Scandal in Bohemia" (2020, MX Publishing)

Murder Most Grotesque: The Comedic Crime Fiction of Joyce Porter (2021, Level Best Books)

Novels:

Sherlock's Secretary (2021, MX Publishing)

Short Story Collections:

Of Course He Pushed Him (2022, MX Publishing)
  (Also available in a two-volume edition.)

Printed in the USA
CPSIA information can be obtained
at www.ICGtesting.com
LVHW050939021223
764722LV00001BA/80